HEWBRIS

# HEWBRIS

## Ian Macpherson

Bluemoose

Copyright © Ian Macpherson 2022

First published in 2022 by
Bluemoose Books Ltd
25 Sackville Street
Hebden Bridge
West Yorkshire
HX7 7DJ

www.bluemoosebooks.com

All rights reserved
Unauthorised duplication contravenes existing laws

British Library Cataloguing-in-Publication data
A catalogue record for this book is available from the British Library

Paperback 978-1-915693-03-7

Printed and bound in the UK by Short Run Press

'The Ancient Greeks have a word for it, Hayding. Hewbris.' – *The three aunts*

*To Davy & Arnold*

# 1

## *Kentish Town. London NW5*

For those wishing to get a comprehensive insight into this historic urban village through the ages, I heartily recommend *The Pubs Beneath*. Old Joanna's gets several mentions. A pretty classy establishment these days, but not when I first arrived in London with sufficient capital for a room in a squat and two pints. In those days, Old Joanna's was strictly spit and sawdust; named after the upright piano that sat semi-upright in one corner, or perhaps the owner, Old Joanna, who sat semi-upright in another. Smoking her Woodbines. Running, it turned out, the empire that cost her a damehood and precipitated her early retirement to Marbella after one turf war too many.

Now? Swish bar with trendy comedy club, The Woom, attached. The Woom sports plush red seats from an old cinema. Aisle up the middle, affectionately known as The Vaj. Blood red carpet, blood red drapes. Performers go in from the bar and stand at the back. Separate door round the side of the building for punters.

That particular evening, as Hayden McGlynn eased open the door from the bar to The Woom, his blood froze. Packed house. Three young women – the Merrie Spinsters – pranced about onstage, singing at full raucous volume. A bawdy ballad by the sound of it. *Polyamóry in Ballydehob.* He caught the odd line – *He died of a heart attack shagging a sheep* – not to mention the odd couplet – *Mr O'Reilly fucked Mrs McCann/When he was a woman and she was a man.*

My comedy guru, Professor Emeritus Larry Stern, has a good deal to say on the first of these in *Bestiality and Necrophilia as Fit Subjects for Comedy*. When he wrote the piece – in 1979 – his take on the subject was irrefutably male. He'd be turning in his grave if he knew that three young women of good upbringing and unimpeachable education would be shamelessly airing such lyrics not half a century later. Assuming he was dead. Which he isn't. We'll draw a discreet veil over the rest of the lyrics, except to say that if your surname is Hadigan, Madigan, Flynn or O'Halloran, Hannigan, Flanagan, Lynch or Magee; or, for that matter, Gilligan, Milligan, Spilligan, Crilligan, Kennedy, Shaughnessy, Doyle or O'Dea, you might wish to take legal advice.

Hayden stood mesmerised in the darkness at the back. Was he really going to be next onstage after *this*? He'd arrived back from Dublin and popped into his old stomping ground for a quick ego massage straight from the airport because he had big, big news, but Bo the compère had nabbed him as he was chatting to Steve the barman. Hot young stand-up Foetus O'Flaherty no show, she'd explained. Would Hayden headline tonight's show instead? No, he wouldn't. End of subject. Absolutely not. To go onstage as the unwanted headliner, when the place had erupted for the previous act, was the stuff of his darkest nightmares; but Bo was very persuasive, and her understated chicken impersonation had swung it, so here he was.

He looked down to check his trousers. He had them on. Well, it was a start, but that's as far as it went. The audience erupted at the end of every verse. They erupted at the end of the song. They erupted at the end of The Merrie Spinsters' triple encore. The ecstatic trio eventually bowed to the inevitable and swept offstage with a triumphant 'Follow that, Foetus!' down through the audience and towards the back door, in front of which stood Hayden: cerebral, tangential, low-key, petrified Hayden. Bit like myself in my stand-up days come to think of it, so I find writing this section particularly difficult. I'm experiencing sympathetic terror.

The women march triumphantly towards Hayden, he sidesteps in time to save his own life, they disappear to the bar area and The Woom is, metaphorically speaking, Mount Vesuvius in full effluvescence. All Foetus O'Flaherty has to do now is ride the wave of molten lava with his cheeky boy charm, the flop of black hair over half his face, and his enormous, seductive, melting left eye. Not to mention his call-and-response catchphrase:

*'Hey fella, where you from?'*

*'Termonfeckin'*

*'Yow!'*

Except that it isn't Foetus. It's Hayden. Cerebral, tangential, low-key, petrified Hayden, with greying hair over neither eye; who'd been tormented, on his last comedic outing, by an unresponsive audience and the fact that his three nonagenarian aunts, who'd phoned him from Dublin mid-set to tell him his Uncle Eddie was dead, had got more laughs than him. Hayden stood waiting as Bo took the mic. Whoops and hollers from the audience. They were ready for the headlining Foetus and they were having a ball. Gig of the century. Woop woop.

Bo raised her free hand and lowered it slowly for calm. More woop woop. Fair enough. Gig of the millennium. Hayden double-checked his trousers. Still on. He'd had time to think this one through. If they hadn't been on he would have woken up at this point. You don't drop in to Old Joanna's, trouserless, in real life. No, this was the real world and Hayden was very much awake.

From the stage, Bo, ever the professional, singled out a particularly boisterous young man for special treatment. 'I shouldn't have to tell you to behave yourself. I'm not your mother.'

'Yes, you are.'

'Funny,' said Bo. 'I don't recall the maternity hospital.'

A loud female voice. 'Layby on the A42, Bo.'

'Ah yes, it's all coming back to me now.'

'You should have left him there, Bo.'

'I did.'

This was getting problematic for Hayden. The audience was enjoying Bo. Worse, it was enjoying itself. Not to mention looking forward to Foetus. Hayden stood frozen. The evening was going brilliantly. Catastrophe.

Bo slotted the microphone back onto its stand. 'Now, speaking of maternity hospitals,' she said, 'Foetus O'Flaherty couldn't be with us tonight. Prior engagement with the labour ward.'

Good line, no laugh. A collective murmur of disapproval. Pivotal moment. The audience had begun to turn. Hayden heard Bo announce his name to a mixture of stunned silence, polite booing, and small pockets of sympathetic applause from fans of the cerebral, the tangential, the high-brow.[1] Give-him-a-chance applause which, in some ways, was worse than none.

He was about to start the long walk to the stage, down the central aisle to his certain comedy death, when his new mantra kicked in: the good news he'd stepped off the plane with earlier that day. The mantra he'd been so desperate to share that he'd come to Old Joanna's straight from the airport. *I'm writing a film script, actually.* He was set on a new, exciting, lucrative path. Stand-up, in world of Hayden, was a thing of the past. He'd get up there. Do his set. Get off. He projected ahead. Oscar speech for best original screenplay. A wave of calm washed over him as he moved forward through the thundering intro music. He was above all this. He was working on a script for the legendary Wolfe Swift, no less. Expecting a call from Wolfe's prestigious agent: screenplays a speciality. He'd also been given the keys to Wolfe's Kentish Town pad while Wolfe spent time in Dublin. *The perfect place to write the perfect script*; Wolfe's parting words. He fingered the keys in his pocket for moral support, breathed slowly in, and strolled casually onstage.

---

[1] See Stern monograph, *A Dying Breed*, for an erudite elegy.

Bo beckoned him graciously into the glare of the spotlight. The music faded out. He removed the microphone and stood holding the stand with one hand, mic cradled lovingly in the other. A man at ease in his own talent, eyes studying the audience with mischievous intent, the merest hint of a smile adding to the pleasingly ironic effect.

He stilled the silent audience, ironically, with his microphone hand, and gestured at the retreating Bo. 'You're *my* mother too,' he said.

Bo turned back. 'Really? And exactly how old are you?'

'Age withheld. But know this. It's every Irishman's fantasy to have a mother who's younger than him.'

Bo laughed. The audience laughed. Hayden felt good, and in comedy, as in life, confidence is all. It was now his to lose. The door at the back opened. The Merrie Spinsters slipped through, drinks in hand. He waved languidly. They gasped in mock shock.

'Jayzus, Foetus, you've aged.'

Hayden was straight in. 'I made the mistake of watching your act.'

The Merries hooted. Excellent. They were onside. He was about to segue neatly into his own act, his new mantra locked firmly in place, when he had an idea. He whipped his mobile out and glanced at the screen.

'Quick check,' he said. 'Expecting a call from Wolfe Swift's agent.'

'Aren't we all, Haydo.' The three Merries in unison.

With the door closed they were in darkness again, but by narrowing his eyes Hayden could make them out at the back of the room. 'You know how it is with actors,' he said. 'They're playing you in a film, they think they own you.'

'He can think he owns us any time, Haydo.'

'So, what's the deal, like? Is he really playing you? Wolfe Swift?'

'Or maybe the boys in the white coats will be bursting through the back door and whisking you off to Planet Delusional.'

That was all three of them. Weird. They spoke in turn, a bit like his three beloved nonagenarian aunts in Dublin. But younger. And they hadn't finished.

'Is there a psychotherapist in the house?'

This wasn't going quite the way Hayden had hoped, but the audience was intrigued. Where *was* he going with this? Hayden wished he knew. Oh, and there *was* a psychotherapist in the house. Two, in fact, sitting in the front row, and they waved at him to continue – they'd started taking notes. Hayden, without knowing it, had checked himself into a session, and he had the perfect joke. 'When I was twelve,' he said, 'I was convinced –'

'– you were Jewish.' The psycho-heckler put her notepad down. 'Classic avoidance technique. Nice try. But Shalom anyway, which means both hello and goodbye, hint-hint.'

'Not strictly accurate.' Her partner scribbled furiously. 'It means peace. Shalom, Hayden. You were saying.'

Hayden worked this through in nanoseconds. His old act was dead. He was wondering where to go next when his mobile rang.

'Jayzus, Haydo. That'll be your new superagent.'

'On you go.'

'Don't mind us.'

The Merries were having a ball. Hayden wasn't. This was spectacularly bad timing. An expectant hush fell as Hayden whipped his mobile out and, too cool to check the caller, answered.

'Howaya, Hayding.'

'Relax.'

'It's only us.'

Hayden's beloved aunts. Bane of his life, and three of the reasons he'd left Dublin to write his screenplay in peace. But maybe their call was no bad thing; they'd phoned him last time he was onstage, the audience response had been orgasmic, and this was one gig he wanted to be done with. Quadruple act with Hayden as straight man? Perfect. He missed the next part of their three-way monologue as he put the phone on speaker.

'Anyway, we were wondering when you were coming over to see your old aunties.'

Their next sentence was drowned out by the roar from the crowd. He raised his hand for silence. 'I've just been over,' he said. 'I kissed you on top of your wizened little heads this very afternoon. Business beckoned. I had to get back.'

'Business beckoned indeed. Pray elucidate.'

'I told you that too,' said Hayden. 'Wolfe Swift? Film script?'

'Oh now, Hayding. Wolfe Swift. The Greatest Actor Of This Or Any Other Age.'

'Tree Oscars and counting.'

'He immersifies, Hayding. That's what puts him ahead of the pack. Total immersification.'

'His ex-wife, whisper it softly, filed for divorce on the grounds that she'd never met him. This-isn't-the-man-I-married type ting.'

'It wasn't eider. He was in character at the time.'

'Henry the 8$^t$.'

'Sadly, she died before the divorce came trew.'

Hayden couldn't help himself. 'He's playing me next, actually,' he said.

'Janey. Two Haydings, Hayding. Is the world ready?'

Hayden sighed theatrically. Of course it was. 'Anyway, I came back to London to finish the screenplay.'

'Reely, Hayding? We tought you were writing a scream of conscience novel.'

The audience hooted. The aunts were on sparkling form. Hayden did the settle down thing with his hand. 'No, no,' he said. 'Back to London. Script. We've been through all this. I asked you to look after Rusty, remember? Eddie's woof-woof?'

'Our dear departed brudder, Hayding.'

'Of course we don't have to tell *you* that. You came over for the funerdle.'

'But a script, dough.'

'Will we be in it?'

'Will we?'

Hayden was happy to change the subject. 'Of course you'll be in it.' He held the phone at arm's length. 'Excellent parts for three minuscule actresses approaching the century mark. Who said there's no great parts for older women?' He clamped the phone back onto his ear. 'Early days yet though, ladies,' he said. 'Bit hush hush.'

'Well, happy scribbling anyway, Hayding. We await your immulent return.'

'My return is far from immulent,' said Hayden. 'I rather fancy I'll be too busy on my burgeoning career in the cinematic arts.'

Rather fancy? Burgeoning? Cinematic arts? Hayden was already distancing himself from mere mortals through the medium of language, and the audience picked up on this. As did the three aunts.

'A word to the wise while you're strutting around over there like a batman cock, Hayding.'

'Hewbris.'

'Hewbris schmewbris, Dottie. Let him have his five minutes.'

'Florrie. And I tought it was fifteen.'

'Well anyway. Rule of tree. Fame. Hewbris. Det.'

'Be warned, Hayding. Or you'll be dead before your time.'

Great exit line.

He put his phone away. Back to solo stand-up. The audience hushed expectantly. Hayden had to think quickly. He couldn't go back into his act now.

Pause. Got it.

'My story,' he began, 'started on this very stage.'

Cue the psycho-hecklers.

'Not so. It started at the moment of conception.'

'Possibly before then. Who can tell?'

Hayden, to wrest control of proceedings, had to tackle them head on. 'I've got twelve minutes max here. Think of this as the edited version. Okay. Backstory. It all started before the moment of conception. It all *continued*' – he paused louchely – 'on this very stage.' Hayden relaxed. The audience fed off his relaxation and settled back. Sometimes it works like that. Besides, he had a story to tell, and what a story. 'I didn't want to be here. I wanted to be at home writing my crime novel, but here I was, going through the motions. Again. I was in the middle of a gag about being convinced I was Jewish –'

'Heard it.'

'Exactly. When my mobile rang.' Long story, but Hayden did a pretty good job of compression:

Travels back to Dublin for his Uncle Eddie's funeral.

Is convinced Eddie, an iconoclastic, heretical artist, has been murdered, but no-one believes him. Becomes the accidental detective.

Discovers Eddie is not his uncle, but his father.

Solves murder.

He included several excellent one-liners and a pretty hilarious take on the three aunts. There was also the delicate matter of the love interest, but he kept that bit to himself. Too painful. He'd reached the denouement of his blackly comic true story, and was about to reveal the identity of Eddie's killer when he stopped suddenly and glanced, theatrically, at his wrist. 'Time flies when you're having fun,' he said. 'You want to find out who did it?'

The psychotherapist duo stopped scribbling. They looked shocked in unison.

'Not *want*, Hayden.'

'*Need*.'

Hayden placed the microphone back into its stand and smirked playfully, a mix of faux and actual smug. 'Go see the movie.' He dropped faux and settled on actual. 'Wolfe Swift *is* Hayden McGlynn. I'll leave it there. Goodnight.'

With that, he was gone. Through the audience and out, the applause and back slaps, not to mention Bo's well-done elbow squeeze on the way past, buoying him up on a wave of love, admiration, and laughter.

# 2

Hayden swung through the bar door and out of The Woom. He may have swaggered over to the counter, where Steve the barman gave him the thumbs up. He was about to order a drink, when the Merrie Spinsters charged out and enveloped him like predatory Amazons.

'That was gas, Haydo.'
'You'd almost think you'd done it before.'
'We particularly liked the three aunts thing.'
'Look no further for the movie.'
'We're like whores round a honeypot.'

Hayden raised a hold-on-a-sec hand. 'Nice idea,' he said, 'if the shoot was delayed, say, sixty years.'

'Come *on*, Haydo. Have you never heard of acting?'

'Vaguely,' said Hayden. 'Another thing. The three aunts are *tiny*.'

'That's the cinematographer's job, Haydo. Long shots.'
'You're floundering, maestro. Listen to this.'
*'Howaya, Hayding.'*
*'Long time no voir.'*
*'Back from Londinium we respectfully opine.'*

Hayden was stunned. A bit of flour in the hair and the Merries *were* the three aunts. Ancient. Wizened. They even appeared to have shrunk several feet. Not to mention the uncanny accuracy of their language. *Voir. Londinium. Respectfully opine.* How did they *know*?

'Don't look so shocked, Haydo. We went to the Holy Fate.'
'It's a select girls' school on your aunties' home patch.'

'Clontarf. You may have ogled the inmates in your youth, Haydo. Unless you're gay.'

'In which case it was ogle the caretaker or get your kicks elsewhere.'

'But we digress. We used to see the three aunts down in Madden's.'

*'Oh now, girls, we will not so buy youze cigarettes.'*
*'You don't want to end up like us.'*
*'In our early tirties and look at us.'*
*'Old before our time.'*

They'd started giggling three aunts-style when the main door opened and Foetus O'Flaherty staggered in. He swayed over to the bar and steadied himself against a stool. He pointed blearily at the row of spirits. Bo was still winding up in The Woom, no-one else to be served, but Steve was busy rearranging his optics; no more drink for Foetus, but he wasn't about to say that – professional ethics. The Merries waved over.

'Will you lookit who it is.'

'Have you met Haydo, Foet? He's a fucking *hoot* for an oul fella.'

'We're playing the three aunts in his movie.'

'And here's a thought. You could play Haydo.'

Try telling that to Wolfe Swift. But Hayden didn't say that. Foetus sat up slightly, a possible expression of interest in his one visible eye. Hayden ruffled his hair. 'Come back when you're born, kiddo,' he said. 'You can play the afterbirth.'

It was meant as a light quip, but that's not how it came out. There was something behind it. The words themselves, the look in Hayden's eyes, suggested a darker subtext, and Foetus, though young and paralytic, was strangely alive to the nuance of language, tone and intent. He stabbed an inebriated finger in Hayden's general direction. A your-card-is-marked-pal finger. Then he folded his arms across Steve's recently polished counter, flopped his head down and fell into a peaceful snore.

As the audience began to pile in from The Woom, the Merries mingled. Hayden braced himself for adulation. It was getting late and he had a script to write, but he could take it. After all, it was the least these good people deserved. As they descended on the bar, however, all eyes were on the sleeping Foetus. His non-appearance, for some reason, had added to his mystique. Bo looked less than delighted to see him, but she had work to do.

'Foetus,' she said. 'Glad you could make it.' Foetus raised his head and tried to focus on her with his one visible, bleary eye. 'Okay,' said Bo, 'now pay attention. See that poster?' She waved a finger at the far wall.

*The Kentish Town International Festival of Comedy*
*The Woom @ OJ's*

She cupped Foetus' head with her free hand and yanked it into position. 'Last day of the festival. Hampstead Heath. Sunday September 27, 3pm. With me so far? All proceeds to the World Peace Foundation.' She glanced across the counter. 'That should do the trick, Steve. No more war.' Back to Foetus. 'Anyway, sure to be a biggie. All-star line-up, few spots left. Nothing to do with me, but your name came up. So, how about it?'

On this occasion, sadly for Foetus, drink overruled ego. 'Ah, fug off,' he slurred, his head sliding back onto Steve's saliva-soaked counter.

'God, you Irish,' deadpanned Bo. 'You are *so sexy*.'

'How about Hayden?' said Steve. 'He's Irish'

Bo squeezed Hayden's arm. 'Sorry, mate. Has to be a name. Love your stuff, but Foetus hot, you not.'

Hayden bridled. Has to be a name? He'd quit stand-up, but this was an affront to his ego, and it seemed the whole bar was listening in. Waiting for a response.

Steve the barman may have sensed his discomfort. 'You probably couldn't get him anyway, Bo,' he said. 'Too busy writing Wolfe Swift's next movie. That right, Hayd?'

Bo thought about this. Wolfe Swift? Point taken. Hayden was now a name by association. She punched him playfully on the arm. 'Done. Ten minutes. Keep it funny. See you there.' She grimaced at the comatose Foetus. 'So sexy. Almost makes me wish I was forty years younger.'

Steve leaned over the counter. 'How old *are* you, Bo?'

'Thirty-nine.'

Hayden's mobile buzzed over the laughter. Caller unknown. Not the three aunts then. Good start. The caller got straight to the point. 'I will be brief, my friend. Present yourself at my business address, tomorrow, at precisely Oh Eight Hundred and Twelve. Is there anything about this message you fail to understand?'

Hayden was momentarily thrown. He opted – the stand-up instinct – for witty. 'And you are?'

'Wolfe Swift told me you are a funny man, Hayden McGlynn. Desist forthwith. If I, Julius Okeke, agree to represent you, *exclusively*, you will have no time for such frivolities as comedy. With Julius Okeke it is strictly business. I hope I have made myself clear.'

As he pocketed his phone, Hayden worked this through. The 'exclusively' word in particular could present a problem. Julius Okele was the agent of every screenwriter's dreams, but Hayden already had an agent: Richard Mann. A crap comedy agent, granted, but an agent is an agent. So, what to do? The answer was simple. Rich was of no further use. He'd dispense with his services. He, Hayden McGlynn, was on the way up and needed a state-of-the-art screenwriting agent to prove it. Several stools further along, self-styled comedy legend Baldy Mayle, alone and unloved, wasn't. He stared into his tankard's dying embers.

'I invented comedy, me,' he said.

Steve shifted Foetus O'Flaherty's head gently and wiped a small pool of saliva from the counter. 'Of course you did, Baldy,' he said absently. 'Of course you did.'

*

As he left Old Joanna's, travel bag hoicked over his shoulder, Hayden clocked a bigger version of the festival poster.

> *The Kentish Town International Festival of Comedy*
> *The Woom @ OJ's*
> *Sept 1-27*

Compère for the duration, Bozienka 'Bo' Bell. Hayden ran his eye down the month-long line-up. Hattie Arbuckle, Les Mahagoe, Paul Muldoonican, Nora Meehan, Susie Quipp, Little Jimmy – Bloody hell! Little Jimmy Lawrie. Stadium filler these days. Bit big for a Woom event? Hayden mentally added his own name at the top of the poster, and turned towards Leverton Street NW, and Wolfe's.

Leverton Street. Hayden had checked the route with Steve the barman. Two-minute walk from the venue, turn left, check the house numbers and there you are. He popped into the local late-night grocer's en route for milk, and was on his way back out when he almost bumped into two young women headed for the flat above the shop.

'Not *want*, Hayden.'

'*Need*.'

He recognised the voices at once. The psychotherapist double act. They fitted together perfectly. Juliette Greco left bank circa 1956 black polo necks. Huge glasses. Short bobs.[2] They needed to know the end of his riveting tale, and there was something about them close up that made him want to confide. He stopped next to the vegetable stand. 'Okay,' he said, 'but

---

[2] Is it just me, or are psychotherapists getting younger?

keep it to yourselves.' He lowered his voice. 'Eddie was not my uncle. The perpetrator was me. Turns out' – he paused here for maximum dramatic effect – 'I killed my father.'

They both looked blank. Double blank.

'Point of information, Hayden.'

'Every man kills his father.'

Hayden snorted. 'I know that,' he said. 'Metaphorically, yes. But I mean literally. Big difference.'

No light of understanding in their eyes. Totally unimpressed.

'History is littered with dead fathers, Hayden.'

'Plus, here's an interesting statistic. In the vast majority of registered cases, fathers predecease their sons.'

Hayden sighed. 'That's because they're older.'

They nodded their heads as if thinking about this. 'Or is it?'

Jesus! Were they serious? Was this where modern psychotherapy had got to post-Freud? And they hadn't finished. 'Thing is, Hayden, it's been done.'

Maybe he should have left it there. He felt a terrible sense of guilt at having killed his own flesh and blood,[3] but he didn't like this, the not getting credit. Patricide passé? Well, how about this? No keep-it-to-yourselves prefix this time; he went straight in. 'I have three mothers.'

Their turn to pause. Double pause. One each.

'Now that is interesting.'

'That is *very* interesting.'

They shoved a card at him.

*Silverman Klein.*
*Our Business, Your Head.*

'We would be keen –'
'Make that *very* keen –'
'– to take this further.'

---

[3] You'll have read about it in *Sloot*. 'A coruscating masterpiece.' – *Hyperbole Now*

'Good to know,' said Hayden. He used the brief distraction of their notebooks being opened to vamoose.

Three mothers! Let *that* ferment in their weird psychotherapeutic brains. Make 'em wait.[4] As he turned the corner into Leverton Street he waved a farewell 'Shalom'.

---

[4] First rule of comedy. There are 27 first rules. This is #9.

# 3

Desirable area. Four-storey terraced house. Wolfe Swift's London pad. The perfect place, he'd told Hayden, to write his breakout script. As Hayden opened the gate to the scrap of front garden, revered comedian Little Jimmy Lawrie came out of a similar house a few doors down, and raced ostentatiously off in a Lamborghini with a personalised number plate: *LJL 1*. Hayden wasn't a Little Jimmy fan, but he liked the Lamborghini and, as he put the key in the lock, the wealth by association. Big moment, this. As he opened the door, Hayden felt like a different person to the one who'd kept the keys to his poky bedsit 'just in case'.

I was reminded of feelgood manual *The Sky's Your Oyster* by positive-thinking guru Joy Bliss. Huge bestseller on publication, although her subsequent descent into chronic depression and suicide hit sales of the 49th, and probably final, print run. At this precise moment, however, the sky was incontrovertibly Hayden's oyster.

Wolfe Swift's house was on the self-same street that I first lived on when I decamped to London all those years ago. I'll go further. It was the self-same house. Mind you, it was a bit less genteel in those days. A run-down squat in a run-down area, but not any more. Hayden stood in the middle of Wolfe's magnificent open-plan ground floor and surveyed it, awestruck, for the first time. He felt at one with the universe. This was what he was born for. Roomy. Luxurious. Perfect London pad for a successful screenwriter, and with Wolfe opting to stay in Dublin for the time being, it almost felt like his own personal property. This – his thoughts danced away with him here – was his destiny! He'd need a pad like this in LA too, but first things first.

As he looked around he noticed a door to the left of the kitchen. Bit like the cellar door at Eddie's in Dublin; the cellar where Eddie had died. The cellar where Hayden – but he didn't want to relive that now. It was still a painful memory and best, perhaps, to leave it for the script. He shuddered and moved away to the back window. Outside, a modest-but-generous-for-London walled garden dotted with plants, and a miniscule-but-generous-for-London area of carefully tended lawn. In front of the window, of all things, a made-to-order writing desk. Very nineteenth century yet totally modern – Davenport's Bespoke Bureaus, for those interested in matters escritoirial – and perfect for Hayden's needs. Almost as if Wolfe had known he'd be inviting Hayden to his house to write his script... but hold on. Wolfe had given Hayden the house key that very morning in Dublin during their first conversation about the script, so how could he possibly have known that Hayden would be writing it there?

Happy chance, then. Happy, happy chance. Yes! This – his feet danced away with him here to mental balalaikas – was indeed his destiny! He draped his jacket over the swivel chair and stood back. It felt, somehow, right. As if the jacket was always meant to be there. He'd get stuck into his script in the morning, when his teeming brain was fully rested and fresh.

Good night's sleep first. Wolfe had mentioned 'a dinky little guest bedroom on the first floor'. He grabbed his bag off the sofa and headed for the stairs, which really were impressive. Steel and glass looking out over the ground floor. You could give a speech from the steps or, if you were a small child, hunker halfway down at night when you couldn't sleep and watch what the adults got up to, undisturbed. Very cinematic. Hayden toyed with the idea of the speech, yawned, then went on his tired but elated way.

First floor. Guest room. Absolutely ideal. Bed made up: hand-plucked, goose down pillow. Silk duvet. Wardrobe. Small table. What Hayden immediately recognised as a Kandinski print on the far wall.[5] Window onto the garden. He tossed his travel bag on the floor and opened the table drawer. No Gideon. Perfect. Busy day, he was exhausted, so he undressed quickly, slipped under the duvet, turned the bedside lamp off, and closed his weary eyes.

Seconds passed. Ten. Twenty tops. His eyes snapped open. The cellar. He'd suddenly thought of the cellar. Not the cellar where Eddie died. Wolfe's cellar. A totally different cellar; nothing to worry about there. And yet. And yet. No way he was getting to sleep till he'd checked it out, so he turned the bedside lamp back on, clambered out of bed, and made his way downstairs. He clicked the living room light on, yawned, and shuffled over to the cellar door. Slightly agitated, not knowing what to expect, he pulled it open and felt for a light switch. Bright white light, unlike Eddie's vermilion. Steep wooden rungs leading down to the cellar, but there the resemblance to Eddie's ended. He ventured down a few steps and looked around. Where Eddie's cellar had been littered with crates of *Sweet Ambrosia*, his homemade apple and pear cider which had almost led to Hayden's ruin, here were tasteful, fitted wine racks. Row upon row of dusty bottles, probably worth a fortune.

It's a little-known fact, but Wolfe Swift had bought the house when the cellar was a disused space between the open-plan floor and the muddy earth beneath. This most secretive of actors used it as background research for his first Oscar-winning role in the one-man period drama, *Priest Hole*. Six months sealed in before he even auditioned. All they found when he finally staggered out was a large sack of monkey nut shells, the original manuscript of *St. Augustine's Confessions*, and the calcified remains of a twelve-year-old choirboy.[6]

---

[5] Kandinski yes, print no.
[6] Okay. Joke. Joke. It wasn't the original.

Hayden stared, mesmerised, at the bottles, remembering his alcohol-fuelled early years with a potent mixture of wistfulness and shame. No, Hayden. No. Career good, alcohol bad. Impending crisis averted, he shuddered and went back upstairs.

He had an important meeting in the morning. Julius Okeke. His soon-to-be new agent. What was it Wolfe Swift had said? *Formality, mate.* All he had to do was sign the contract. What Wolfe Swift wanted, Wolfe Swift got. One final thought as Hayden's head hit the hand-plucked, goose down pillow. He wanted a house like this. Wanted? *Needed.* Move over Richard Mann. He'd seen the future, and the future was money. The future was Hayden. The future was success.

# 4

Julius Okeke sat behind his magnificent oak desk by a huge window, overlooking a sun-dappled Regent's Park. And Julius was as impressive as the view. Three-piece pinstripe. Gold cufflinks. Matching fob.

Eight eleven: Julius on the phone.

Eight twelve: Julius off the phone.

He removed the watch from his waistcoat and flicked it open. 'You are a punctual man, Hayden McGlynn. This pleases me. Wolfe Swift speaks highly of you. This also pleases me. He wishes to make a film of your story. So. You have ninety seconds precisely.' He clicked his watch and waited.

Hayden breathed in deeply. He hadn't been expecting this. *Formality, mate*? He exhaled and checked his watch. Ninety seconds. Okay, but where to start? 'Long story short,' said Hayden. 'Our hero, let's call him Hayden.'

'Interesting name,' said Julius Okeke. 'Describe to me this Hayden.'

Hayden hadn't been expecting this either. Did ninety seconds include interruptions? 'Well,' he said. 'Bit like me.'

'Excellent description,' said Julius. 'I see him clearly. Proceed.'

Hayden looked at Julius. Was he joking? Hard to tell. He proceeded. 'His three nonagenarian aunts phone from Dublin when he's onstage. Comedy club, tough gig, and he'd much rather be at home writing his crime novel, so he takes the call.'

'Already I see these three ancients,' said Julius. 'The Greek chorus. The three witches in *Macbeth*.' He dropped his voice.

'The fates. Yes, I begin to get a feel for this. Its depth. Its complexity.'

Good to know, Julius, but what? Sixty seconds left? On with the narrative. 'His Uncle Eddie has just died.' You don't have to see Uncle Eddie, Julius. He's dead. Hayden kept that bit to himself. 'Hayden goes to Dublin for the funeral, but something's not right. Has Eddie been murdered? No-one else thinks so, or so they say, so Hayden becomes the accidental detective. He soon has a list of suspects, including the detective inspector who should be solving the case but isn't, and Marina, who may be running a house of ill repute from this most sedate of –' Hayden faltered. He was suddenly overcome with a wave of unbidden emotion. Bad, bad timing. '– of suburbs. Turns out she's not a – she's – sorry, it's…'

Marina, it had turned out, was a psychotherapist, and Hayden, in spite of himself, had been – and remained – smitten. She'd offered him a double session. He'd assumed – but maybe he was wrong. Maybe he'd misinterpreted 'double session'. She was, after all, off work when she said it. Could it be that she, too, had been smitten?

'You are a man of great feeling,' said Julius Okeke. 'This Marina. The love interest, yes?' Hayden, unable to speak, nodded. Marina, the woman he'd left behind. The love interest, *yes*, and she didn't even know it. Julius smiled softly. 'You have the gift, Hayden McGlynn. I see this woman in my mind's eye. Sherilee Lewis.[7] But do go on.'

Sherilee Lewis? Marina? Some mind's eye you've got there, Julius, thought Hayden, but ninety seconds, probably down to twelve, so he wound it up. 'The crime is solved, but not in the way he'd anticipated.'

'Don't tell me,' chuckled Julius, 'or I won't, as our American friends so eloquently put it, go see the movie.'

---

[7] Actress. Interesting choice.

Was Julius Okeke playing with him? Hayden really couldn't tell, so he raced towards the denouement. 'The outcome of Hayden's accidental investigation leads him into a spiral of existential despair, but when things can't get any worse, he's overheard by the hugely celebrated actor, Wolfe Swift, as he pours out his tragic story in the local bar. Wolfe is transfixed. *What a story, what a twist. My people, your people.* Hayden is back on top. He's got his crime idea, except it's not a novel after all, it's a film, and Wolfe Swift – the hottest property in cinema – is going to play the lead. Celtic screwball noir. Happy ending. Credits.'

'Eighty-seven seconds,' said Julius Okeke. 'Room for expansion, but well done.' He pressed his long fingers together and ruminated. Thinking done, he sat back and studied Hayden. '*My people, your people,*' he said. 'I, Julius Okeke, am Wolfe Swift's people. My question to you, Hayden McGlynn, is this: who is, or are, *your* people?'

Hayden was thrown. 'Ah yes, well –'

Julius Okeke cut across his confusion. 'Because if I am to represent you, we must be clear on one thing. *I* am your people. Thou shalt not have false people before me. Sole representation, as previously mentioned. Understood?'

Hayden sat up. Sole. As in 'exclusive'. 'Oh, right,' he began. 'See, the thing is –'

Julius Okeke wagged a long finger. 'No, my friend, the thing is not. When someone says to me the thing is, I know exactly what that thing is. And I say to you now, that thing must not be.' He drummed his fingers on the mighty oak. 'You are currently represented. That much is clear. Name?'

Hayden had a bad feeling about this. A sense of foreboding. He dropped his eyes. And his voice. 'Richard Mann?'

Julius drummed faster. 'Well then,' he said, 'we have a mutual problem. You wish to know what that problem is? It is Richard Mann. Richard Mann is a problem, but Richard Mann is also a test.' Julius paused for effect. 'There is an old saying which I learned growing up in Matabeleland: *He owns you, therefore you must kill him and let me own you.* But be discreet. And remember, we must always respect our prey, even as we kill them.'

Hayden thought about laughing, but that didn't seem to be the desired response. Bit of a problem if he did and it wasn't, so instead he tried, 'Sorry, I don't quite follow.'

Julius Okeke leaned back in his chair and clasped his hands behind his head.

'It is simplicity itself. I need to know how much you want this.' He paused again. Three seconds. Maybe four. 'You must extricate yourself from Richard Mann, you must do it ruthlessly, and you must do it with immediate effect.'

'B-but –'

Hayden stuttered to a halt.

Julius Okeke stared at him. Four seconds. Maybe five. He then checked his contact list, lifted the landline, dialled, put the phone on loudspeaker, and passed it to Hayden. Rich answered immediately. Julius Okeke's number. Important Call. Rich was always there for an Important Call.

'Julio! My main man.'

Julius arched an eyebrow as Rich's voice trilled from the loudspeaker. Bright. Keen. Almost, you'd be forgiven for thinking, deferential.

'It's not Julio, Rich. It's Julius. And it's not Julius. It's Hayden.'

Rich's tone frosted over. Deference fled. 'You're in a bad place, Ay. Something you'd like to share?'

Hayden made eye contact with Julius. 'I'm leaving you, Rich,' he said.

Julius smiled encouragingly. Good opener.

'Straight to the point, Ay.' Rich's voice sounded distant and tinny now. 'But will it work? Let me mull it over. Nah. No can do, Ay. Small matter of the contract, see? You're my pension plan. Well, you and several others. It's a till-death-do-us-part type thing, compren? Right, I'm off for a quick –'

'Whoa,' said Hayden. 'We have to –'

'We 'ave to nothing, Ay,' said Rich, an undertone of malice seeping in. 'You know the my-people-your-people schtick? *I'm* your people. Never forget that.'

Hayden shifted uneasily in his seat. 'Sorry, can we wind it back a bit there, Rich? This contract –'

'Sitting in front of me even as we speak. You know what they say. Keep your clients close, keep your contracts closer.'

'But… I don't remember any contract.'

'Course you don't. Get 'em young, see? *Sign here, mate*, so you did. Too busy jerking off about your brilliant career to check the small print.' Rich snorted happily. 'Your brilliant career, Ay. Ever wonder what 'appened to that?'

'Well then,' said Hayden, 'you'll be glad to see the back of me. Good result all round.'

Julius smiled enigmatically. Back to Rich. 'I think you may be forgetting our motto, Ay. *We never let go*. That, my friend, is what makes us great.'

The buzz of the dialling tone filled the room. Julius Okeke stroked his chin with a meditative finger and gazed, inscrutably, at Hayden. The your-move gaze. Hayden looked away. 'I'm sure we can come to some arrangement,' he mumbled over the dialling tone, as he handed the phone back to Julius.

Julius examined the mouthpiece as if looking for clues, then placed it gently back in its cradle. 'Come back and see me when you are a free man, Hayden McGlynn,' he said. 'It is now oh eight seventeen.' The phone rang. He waited a moment – 'oh eight eighteen' – and lifted the receiver. 'Meryl,' he said. 'Good of you to call.'

And he waved Hayden out with a languid hand.

\*

I recently decided to buy a book to remind me of my magical years in London and opted, finally, for the London A-Z. Hayden was making his way back to Wolfe's along my favourite page:

forty-five. Kentish Town Road: I name you for the blessed memories of a gloriously misspent decade. All changed now and yet, somehow, all exactly the same. Bo Bell was about to pop into one of the more recent additions, Intersects, when she spotted Hayden thundering along the footpath on his way back to Wolfe's.

'Great face for comedy,' she said. 'Undertaker, no clients.'

Hayden scowled at her, then softened and slowed to a halt. 'Fucking agents,' he said.

Bo linked her arm through his. 'Come with Bo,' she said. 'You need a stiff coffee.'

She wheeled him in through the bespoke bookshop door. Lovely shop. Books, obviously. Café section: Browse & Quaff. Probably part of a chain, but it certainly looked enticing. Bo settled Hayden into a seat, ordered coffees and brought them to the table. On a tray. With a dinky little bowl of brown and white sugar lumps. She sat down and took a quick sip of her double espresso. Hayden pulled his cup towards him, plucked a brown sugar lump from the bowl and rolled it meditatively between his thumb and middle finger, like a dice. Bo smiled inscrutably. 'Fucking agents, quote unquote,' she said. 'Any particular one?'

'That's the problem,' said Hayden. 'I've got two.'

'Ah.'

'Exactly.'

Bo nodded her head with the wisdom of lived experience. 'They both want you all to themselves. Bit like a love triangle without the love. So let's do a personality profile on both parties and see where that gets us.'

'Fair enough,' said Hayden, absently crumbling the sugar lump into his cup and stirring gently. 'Julius Okeke.'

'Really?' said Bo. 'As in *I'm writing a film script, actually* stroke *expecting an important call from my new agent* stroke *Wolfe Swift is playing me, actually.* That one?'

Hayden shrugged modestly.

'I'm impressed,' said Bo. 'Wolfe Swift *is* Hayden McGlynn. I hope he gets that thing you do with your – forget it. Okay. Julius Okeke. So far, so top of the range. You said two.'

Hayden chose another sugar lump, white this time. No rolling, he crumbled it violently onto his saucer. 'Richard Mann.'

'Double Ah. He tried to sign *me* up,' said Bo. 'And other things.' She grimaced at the memory. 'My advice? Never sign anything. Always carry a mallet in your purse.' She patted Hayden's arm. 'I take it you fell for his seductive charms and whipped out your Bic.'

'Close enough,' winced Hayden. 'It was a Rollerball.'

He chose two sugar lumps this time, one for each hand.

'Well, that's you tied up for life.' Bo stifled a laugh. 'Sorry, shouldn't have put it like that. Bit of a Richism. You know. Given his proclivities.' She suddenly lit up. 'Hold on though. Let me get this straight. You're with Rich. You lust, artistically speaking, after Julius. That about it?'

'Pretty much. So?'

'Elementary, my dear Hayden. Rich is your comedy agent. I thought you'd given up on the stand-up. Well, give or take a World Peace Foundation ego-fest. Julius Okeke is film. So kill the comedy. Embrace the Oscar acceptance speech.'

Hayden sat with his mouth open. Brilliant. Why hadn't *he* thought of that? 'You're a miracle, Bo,' he said.

Bo waved the compliment away. 'It's a gene thing,' she said. 'I take no personal credit.' She drained her cup and placed it back on the saucer. 'Right,' she said. 'Productive quaff. Time to browse.' She stood up. 'Problem solved, no charge. See you on the red carpet.' She turned to go, then turned back. 'Oh, and by the way, I'd go easy on the sugar. That Best Screenplay Oscar? You'll need your teeth for the speech.'

# 5

Have I mentioned my own scriptwriting? I've written quite a few over the years. Haven't had a great deal of success so far. Okay, so this book is about Hayden, not me, but my point is, I know how to write 'em. Structure. Character arc. Dialogue. All the technical stuff. I've still got a folder full of industry pitches. Quick example:

> *Jonah Whale* 'A bittersweet movie about a comedian on the skids who has a surprise Edinburgh Festival hit with a 'moving-yet-hilarious' show about the death of his father. The following year it's his mother's turn. When all four siblings die in mysterious circumstances, coinciding with his third sell-out appearance to ecstatic reviews, the term Misery Mirth is born. But is there more to these convenient tragedies than meets the eye?'
>
> 'A masterpiece of exhilarating wokeness' – *The Guardian*

Forget the quote. I added that as an ironical comment on its not-madeness. And misery comedy didn't even exist at the time. But as I say, this is not about me, it's about Hayden.

He'd started the script in Dublin, and seemed to be on top of the technical aspects. I think they teach that sort of stuff in nursery these days. The plotline was straight from life, so no problems there; characters, story, startling revelations all in place, waiting to be written down as lived.

# BAD BLOOD

by

Hayden McGlynn

Hayden sat hunched over the screen, tap tapping. The script poured out onto his laptop. Sad news: Eddie dead. Return to Dublin. Dawning realisation: Eddie murdered. He slowed up for the perpetrator's unmasking. More than that, he wept – always a good sign – as he relived the traumatic experience for the screen version. Particularly as he discovered he'd murdered Eddie himself and that Eddie was his father. Which explained the script's heartbreaking Dark Night of the Soul sequence. Then? Meeting the legendary Wolfe Swift at the Nautical Buoy pub. Success!

There was something pleasingly meta about the story. Hayden looking for a crime novel in his imagination and other people's books, but finding it in the real world instead. This allowed him to put in a sub-plot involving his childhood friend Bram, the talk-to guy, and Bram's new love, Trace – who also happened to be Hayden's self-styled AA minder. A subversion of the romantic comedy genre, where the wrong guy gets the wrong girl, and they live happily ever after. Which brought him to Marina. He was the right guy, she was – she was – enough, Hayden. Pack it away. Move on. Back to the script.

Good enough for a first draft. The end, however, needed to be a bit – what's the word? – *oomphier*. The final scene where Hayden met Wolfe Swift in the pub felt a little flat to Hayden, somehow. Still, it wasn't bad. Not bad at all. Well, apart from the dreaded voiceover. But we'll get to that later.

Hayden, meanwhile, closed his laptop with a contented sigh and headed for the great outdoors.

# 6

Hampstead Heath was a brisk twenty-minute walk from Wolfe's. Two inches in my London A-Z. Hayden stood at the summit of Parliament Hill and breathed in the clear, clean air of this bracing September morn. A few kites wafted about, autumnal colours adding a melancholy beauty to the scene. A superannuated kite-flyer was having some trouble controlling his instrument and the kite, a red, green and gold phoenix, strained at the leash and pulled him this way and that like an excited pup. Beneath this painterly vista, spread out in all its glory, the fume-tinged majesty of the throbbing metropolis. Forgive the hyperbole, and sorry to harp on about it, but I first stood atop Parliament Hill in mid-September many years ago, and the memory affects me still. In my mind's eye it resembles, from this most pleasing of vistas, a masterpiece by that great landscape painter, Turner.

Or is it Constable?

Hayden was trying to access a few lines by the immortal Wordsworth – the view has that sort of effect – when his mobile rang. The meditative peace of the morning shattered. Tranquillity fled. Hayden shouted into the mouthpiece to counter the blustery breeze. 'Rich!'

The kite flyers avoided his gaze. Gentle philosophers all, they hated mobile phones and regarded their users with a deep, and potentially violent, gun-lobby loathing.

'Top gig, Ay,' said Rich. 'Largs. You'll be supporting –'

Hayden snorted with dismissive glee. 'You don't get it, do you, Rich? You're off the case. I'm not a stand-up any more. You're not my agent. And Largs? Supporting? Top gig?'

'Joke, Ay. Oh, and word has it you're writing a script for Wolfe Swift. Fing is, we've got you stitched up, old son. We being me.'

Hayden sighed the do-I-have-to-explain-everything-in-words-of-one-syllable sigh. 'Let me explain something,' he roared into the phone. 'You, comedy agent. Julius, screen agent. Comedy? The past. Screen with, I imagine, offshore-account-loads of lovely spondulicks? The future. We're talking about me here, by the way. *Rich.*'

'Fair dos, Ay, but for the small matter of contract involving Rich, *aka* me, *aka* – and here's the relevant bit as far as our future together is concerned – Richard Mann @ TLM. Let me put that in layman's language, Ay. You came to me as a young gag merchant, eager for success. I opened doors for you. I pointed you in the right direction. I got you that all-important first gig in – where was it again?'

'Largs?'

'Nice one. Gravesend, that was it. I nurtured you, Ay. Ipso facto pardon-my-French? There has to be something in it for me, Ay. A quid, if you like, pro quo. Emphasis, pun intended, on the quid.' There was something about his skittish tone that rang warning bells with Hayden. Rich seemed pretty sure of himself. Then again, didn't agents always? 'Still there, Ay?'

'Hanging on your every word, Rich.'

'So, TLM. Ever wondered what it stands for?'

Hayden braced himself. He had a bad feeling about this. 'Surprise me,' he said, hoping to keep it lighter than he felt.

'Oh, I will, Ay. Triple Lock Management. We've got you tied up, Ay. Every way you look. Stand-up. Scripts. You can't even take a crap without permission. It's all right there in your contract.' Sound of rustling in the background. 'Ciao, mate. You have a very pleasant day now.'

Hayden pocketed his phone and stayed rooted to the spot where I had stood all those years ago. But Turner? Constable? Hayden's mental image, as London lay before him in all its rapacious venality, now looked more like William Hogarth. High above the insatiable metropolis he spotted the phoenix, flailing about in a sudden gust, the taut strings knotting in the kite flyer's fingers. As Hayden watched, the kite soared unexpectedly, flailed again, then plummeted to earth. Alive to the possible symbolism, he pocketed his mobile and headed down the hill.

\*

Hayden had a bad night's sleep. Goose down pillows were no comfort to him now. This was compounded, next day, by a text from his childhood friend Bram as he sat outside a burger bar munching on a big something.

*Dublin is so, so proud.*

No hint of irony – Bram didn't run to irony. Hayden hadn't even finished the script yet, let alone accepted the Oscar screenwriting gong. Big mistake sharing your anticipated success with your friends.

A couple of pigeons landed on a nearby plastic table as he thought up a witty response. Tough one. He'd got as far as *Thanks* when an old woman sat down next to him, opened her bag and started fumbling inside. Hayden glanced over. She had a kindly, open face, the sort you confide in without thinking. Maternal. It's a quality you don't often find in men. She beamed at Hayden. What is it, dear? She didn't say this. Her beam suggested it, but Hayden's thoughts were concentrated elsewhere. Not so much on the follow-up to *Thanks*, but on his present predicament. The question of what to do next.

He was brought back to reality by a voice coming as if from afar. 'You mustn't agonise so.' Did the old lady say that? Or had he flipped over into psychosis? But no, because here she was again. 'In my experience, dear, all men kill their fathers. Agents not so much, statistically, but what do statistics know?'

Hayden looked at her in shocked disbelief. Had he been thinking about killing Rich? Worse, had he said it all out loud? He pressed send on *Thanks* and studied her kindly face. The pigeons fluttered over to his table and studied her kindly face as well. She continued to fumble.

'Thing is,' he said. 'I'm tied into this contract with Rich for life.'

'Life?' she beamed. 'Puff. It's here then it's gone.'

She was right. The old lady was right. Hayden needed to work this through. 'Julius Okeke,' he said.

'Yes, dear? What about him?'

Hayden answered as if he was talking to himself. As if the old woman already knew his thoughts. 'Let me give you this verbatim. *He owns you, therefore you must kill him and let me own you.* I mean, what exactly did Julius *mean* when he said that?'

*He* was asking *her*? But it seemed somehow right. She put the question back to him. 'What do you think he meant, dear?'

'I think he meant, *You must extricate yourself from Richard Mann, you must do it ruthlessly, and you must do it now!*' He looked at the old lady for guidance. She continued to beam, fumbling all the while in her bag. A few more pigeons fluttered down onto Hayden's table. He was about to shoo them off but something told him not to. 'He was probably speaking metaphorically,' he said. It sounded a bit limp, but the old lady oozed empathy.

'Quite possibly, dear,' she beamed, 'but how do you kill someone metaphorically?' Her beam metamorphosed into a warm, endearing chuckle. 'And besides, what good would that do anyway? Would it solve your problem? Would it ease your mental torture? Would it allow you, dear, to move on?'

Good questions. Excellent questions. Would it, would it, would it? How Hayden wished he knew. As he struggled to answer these questions in his own mind, the old lady whipped her hand from her bag and tossed an old-lady-fistful of tiny bread squares, like edible confetti, into the lowering sky. The air suddenly darkened with dive-bombing birds. She tossed another handful, and patted Hayden gently on the arm. 'I killed my husband, dear,' she said, beaming happily at the memory as the hordes came in to land. 'He was the sweetest, kindest, gentlest man.' Pause, as she was enveloped in fluttering wings, for a contented sigh. 'I suppose I just fancied a change.'

# 7

*How shall I kill thee?*
*Let me count the ways.*

Shakespeare? Donne? One or the other. There are probably dozens of ways to murder someone. Unfortunately, Hayden couldn't think of any that suited his particular skillset. He'd killed his father, but that had been an unconscious act. Hadn't it? Hayden's thoughts here.

*I mean, I'd been totally stocious at the time. Perhaps that's the secret. Do it without knowing it. I got away with it the first time, so why not stick to a winning formula?*

Murder by accident? Was such a thing possible? No, Hayden had to face it, he'd simply hit lucky first time. He felt a sharp pang of guilt as he thought this. He'd killed his father. He hadn't meant to kill him. It wasn't his fault it had all the makings of a hit film. Rich, on the other hand, was an insoluble problem. What was needed was a deus ex machina, but how often does one of those come along? The alternative, he supposed, was for someone who was even more upset with Rich than he was to do the job for him. Rich's mother? Wife? Husband? Father? Sibling? Unlikely. Rich lived for his work. Office/Home. Same place. So it would have to be a client. Back to Hayden. He was now engaged in circular thinking, and that way madness lies.

As if to taunt him, everything else was going so well. He loved his new address. He still got the Wow! feeling every time he walked through the front door. *Bad Blood* had stood up to a second reading. Bit ropey in places, and I've mentioned the dreaded voiceover. Example:

SCENE 12. INT. EDDIE'S BUNGALOW. DAY.

Hayden opens door to cellar and peers in.

HAYDEN (V/O) I opened the door to the cellar and peered in.

See? Totally unnecessary. Cut. But otherwise a halfway decent draft. Except, as I've said, for the final scene. Meeting Wolfe Swift in the Nautical Buoy and getting the film script offer; was it too – static? Hayden understood this on a subliminal level. What was that word again? *Oomph!* He settled down at the writing desk to brood. It took his mind off –

Aha! He'd put his two problems together. Script ending, killing Rich. Thanks to his 'fucking agent' – the two words seemed to be made for each other – he now had the consummate, deeply satisfying climax, fuelled by cold rage. He started typing furiously. Last scene: after meeting Wolfe Swift and agreeing to write a film script for him about Eddie's murder, Hayden leaves the Nautical Buoy, phones his soon-to-be-ex-agent when he gets outside and rants into his mobile. Hayden typed feverishly, a word-for-word replay of what had happened in real life:

RICH: (ANSWERPHONE) *Can't get to the phone at the moment. It's in my pocket but I'm all tied up. Leave a message if you think you're important.*

HAYDEN: (WAITS FOR BEEPS) *Just a quickie, Dickie. Can't do the tour.*

HAYDEN: (AS RICH) *Why's that, Ay?*

HAYDEN: (AS HAYDEN) *Well, Dickie, it's like this. Too fucking busy. Wolfe Swift, Rich. Heard of him? Irish 'fillum' actor. Six Oscars. Wants to shoot my script.*

HAYDEN: (AS RICH) *Sweet, Ay. Now here's how we play it.*

HAYDEN: (AS HAYDEN) *We? Nah, Dickie. Here's how I play it. First fillum,* Bad Blood. *Not about us, Dickie, so relax. For now. Follow up.* Rich Mann, Dead Mann. *Our hero – that's me, Rich – kills his agent. That's you, Rich. No idea how to do it yet, but don't worry. Hate will find a way.*

END CALL. HAYDEN DANCES HOME TRIUMPHANT.

Perfect! Hayden had managed to kill Rich without killing him. A bloodless catharsis. That was one of his two problems solved, at least – the script had its *oomphier* ending.

The euphoria wouldn't last forever, though – Rich was, of course, still alive, and still very much a problem – but for now Hayden felt like celebrating a great ending to a great script. And good God, was that the time?! Funny how it speeds by when you're deep in the muse. He closed his laptop, grabbed his jacket and headed out. A trip to the late show at Old Joanna's. Might catch a couple of acts. Might wait till the show was over and mingle.

Truth was, he had no intention of catching a couple of acts. He'd cut straight to mingle. 'I've just finished a film script, actually.' He hadn't, actually. He'd written a serviceable draft. With voiceover. But thinking about his new and brilliant career drove all thoughts of Rich and his accursed Triple Lock Management out of Hayden's head. For now. He checked himself in the kitchen wall mirror and stepped out into the night.

\*

The bar, when Hayden entered, was almost empty. A few people he didn't recognise, and Baldy. Same seat. Different empty glass.

Hayden sauntered over to Steve, who was slowly pouring a pint. Steve nodded towards The Woom. 'They're all in there,' he said. 'Soon as Lenny went up.'

Lenny Broonstein. The world's angriest man. Hayden liked a bit of angry. Preferably vicarious. He found it curiously soothing. 'Might check him out,' he said, moving towards the door. 'Finished the script, by the way. Lookin' good.'

Hayden could hear raucous noise from The Woom. Lenny Broonstein spewing bile. By the sound of it he was well into his signature rant, *Ah Hate*, bullets of spit splattering the back wall as he worked his way up from rage and bile to incandescence. Hayden was already halfway through the door when Steve, placing the pint on the spill tray, called after him. 'Pretty heavy stuff about your old mate Rich.'

If Hayden heard him he didn't acknowledge it. He slipped inside and quietly closed the door. Lenny was, in the parlance of the comedy world, on fire. Wielding the mic stand like a weapon. Ranting.

*Ah hate black people, white people, people wi' wee pink spotties.*
*Ah hate the Twa Corbies, the Three Wise Men, the Four Horsemen o' the Apocalypse.*
*Ah hate Five Guys Named Fuckin Mo.*
*Ah hate people who dinnae ken the Twa Corbies. Ignorant cunts.*
*Ah hate Stanley Crapp o' 12b Mingin Avenue, Scunthorpe. No particular reason. Ah picked the name at random from the darker recesses o' ma sick fuckin heid. Oh, an tek the Shorpe out o' Scunthorpe, whit's left? CUNT!*
*Aye. CUNT!*
*Ah hate cunts on modest wee incomes an' it's a modest wee hoose but we've managed to pay the mortgage aff and we're rather prood o' that cuz we're*
*SMUG WEE FUCKIN' SHITES.*
*Ah hate rich cunts, cunts called Rich.*

*Ah hate Irish cunts, English cunts, cunts from anywhere cunts.
Ah hate everybody. Ah hate everything*

<small>– although I quite like butterflies! –</small>

*but above all ah hate people who pretend tae be fae Glesga
WHEN THEY WANT TAE SOUND AGGRESSIVE!!!*

Lenny flung the mic stand down and stormed off. The place went wild. Bo Bell, back onstage, applauded him on his way and rode out the wave of hysteria. Her mic-free hand descended slowly, almost meditatively, to suggest calm, tranquillity, repose. Peace descended. Slowly. Meditatively. Calmly. 'Now as you all know,' she began, 'we don't do censorship here, but in case you've pre-booked to see –'

A distraught audience member cut across her. 'Oh *no*, Bo. Don't tell us he's had to cancel *again*.'

''Fraid so,' said Bo. 'Next week's headliner was supposed to be King of the Rape Joke, Little Jimmy Lawrie.' She snuffled playfully and wiped away a tear of compassion. 'Tragically, he was butt-fucked on the way here by a coach-load of over-zealous fans, which should give him plenty of new material when he finally gets out of intensive care. So get well soon, Little Jimmy, and do lighten up. As you say yourself in your nod to the great philosopher Jeremy Bentham: Gang rape – the greatest happiness for the greatest number. There's always one gainsayer. In this case, happily, you.' Bo slotted the mic back in the stand. 'Short break,' she said. 'Back in ten.'

Hayden stood where he was as the audience filed excitedly out. Lenny was on form, shame about poor little gang-raped Jimmy, but –

*Pretty heavy stuff about your old mate Rich.*

Steve's words had finally filtered through.

*

The bar was six deep. Steve was in his element. Hayden waved to get his attention from the back of the queue. 'Rich,' he shouted. 'What about him?' Steve poured a pint with one hand and ran a finger across his neck with the other. Hayden didn't follow. 'Sorry?!'

Steve was a great barman. Clean counter, ability to clock who was next in line at a crowded bar, philosopher, confidante, friend. But even Steve, with extra bar staff, couldn't cope with the sudden interval rush *and* a casual chat with Hayden. No time for anything more than a finger across the neck. That gesture usually meant one thing, but what were the chances of that? There was no God,[8] and even if there was, He, She, They or It was hardly likely to be looking out for Hayden's best interests. One way to check, though. Hayden squeezed through the crowd and took his mobile outside. That was better. It was cold and dark, with drunks swaying past or into OJ's, but at least Hayden could hear himself think. He tapped in Rich's number.

*'Can't get to the phone at the moment. It's in my pocket but I'm all tied up. Leave a message if you think you're important.'*

It didn't sound like it came from beyond the grave. Hayden was about to go back inside when an inebriation of off-duty comics reeled past him towards the entrance. Hattie Arbuckle. Les Mahagoe. Nora Meehan. Paul Muldoonican. Izzy Edwards. Susie Quipp. Interesting that they were the very ones I name-checked earlier. Oh, and Jimmy Clitoris. Interesting, also, how many comedians are called Jimmy. This particular specimen was about to land the lead in the hit transgender sitcom, *Meet the Midwife*, but he didn't know that yet. Hayden caught the conversation as they went in.

'*I* killed him.'

'No you didn't, you cunt. *I* killed him.'

'Motive?'

'He didn't take me on. Yours?'

---

[8] Note to all true believers: Relax. Good news pending. Chapter 16 for details.

'He did.'

And in they went, hooting.

Hayden tried the number again. Still tied up. He pocketed the phone and went back inside. Noise. Bustle. People, people, people. He weaved his way over to the bar, where Bo was biding her time on a barstool, surrounded by shouting comedians.

Hayden held up his mobile. 'My ex-agent,' he yelled. 'Rich. He's not answering his phone.'

'I'm not surprised,' said Bo. 'All things considered.' She smiled and glanced at her watch. 'Good timing for you, though. Right. Back to work.' She put her glass down. 'Play nicely, people. Don't kill anyone I wouldn't.'

Steve accepted a contactless payment and waved her off with his other hand. He motioned for Hayden's phone. Hayden passed it over, and as the audience started to file back into The Woom, Steve scrolled down the screen till he found what he was looking for. He handed it back to Hayden. A breaking news headline: *Top agent found dead. Detective Chief Inspector Ronnie Pointer, Camden Met, doesn't rule out accidental suicide.*

Hayden stared at the tiny screen. 'Bloody hell,' he said. The screen went dark and he tapped it again to stare at it a moment longer. 'Bloody *hell*.' But it couldn't be true. Could it? Rich dead? He felt a sharp pang of loss. Involuntary, maybe, but death has that effect. He was processing this counter-intuitive response, and waiting for Steve to finish serving a customer, when the main door opened and Foetus O'Flaherty staggered in. He wound his unimpeded way to the bar and flung a limp arm round Hayden. 'How's it going, ole buddy ole pal?' he said. 'No hard feelings, hoh? You and me. Me and you. We're... Lemme put it this way. I do commo. You used to do commo. Seen you up there on stage. Not bad. Not bad. Thing is, ole bully ole pad, we're both part of the great... Jaze, it's a beautiful fucking world.'

He lurched over to The Woom entrance, fumbled with the door for a while, managed to open it and fell inside. Steve used a brief lull to lean into the counter. 'What's eating *him*?' he said.

Hayden's response was drowned out by audience chants from the heart of The Woom as they spotted Foetus.

*'Hey fella, where you from?!'*

*'Termonfeckin!'*

*'Yow!'*

The Foetus O'Flaherty call and response catchphrase. Delivered with an almost religious intensity by an ecstatic crowd. Hayden looked over at the door. Normally he'd be furious – Foetus wasn't even *performing* – but this wasn't normally. His initial grief at the death of a fellow human being, any human being, had given way, via relief, and guilt at feeling relief, to a mellow inner glow. He was a free man. Steve placed a bottle of sparkling water on the counter and filled a glass with ice and lemon. He placed it on a beer mat and slid it across to Hayden.

'A sad day,' said Hayden, lifting his glass. 'A sad, sad day. Cheers.'

# 8

Hayden bought milk and hot chocolate at the late-night grocers on his way back to Wolfe's. Settled in with a steaming mug, he had a quick look at the last scene of his *Bad Blood* script for the sheer pleasure of reliving it. *END CALL. HAYDEN DANCES HOME TRIUMPHANT.* Hallelujah! Sympathy for the deceased had now given way to euphoria. Three mugs of hot chocolate later, he slept the sleep of the innocent. And he *was* innocent, no question. He'd killed Eddie, but he hadn't killed Rich. It was almost as if one cancelled out the other. He'd atoned for one murder by not committing another.

He awoke refreshed, and whistled Mozart's *Requiem* with gusto as he shaved. He hummed the sad bit from Mahler's *Fifth* as he filled a celebratory kettle. The happy version. Happy doesn't work with Mahler, but who cares? To the happy person, all is happiness. And Hayden was happy. More than happy, he was positively trippy.

Hayden waltzed over to his laptop to the dying strains of *Allegri Miserere*, jollified to suit. He flicked, again, to the last few pages of his script. Slight tweak. Our hero now skips gaily homewards to the joyous strains of Monteverdi's *Lamento della Ninfa*. The Whistling Postman cover. Still perfect. Possibly even more so.

Hayden thought about his deceased ex-agent as he waited for the kettle to boil. Empathetically? In deepest sympathy with his grieving family? Not really. They, too, had been tied to a contract for life. They were probably relieved to get out of it. No. His thinking about Rich had more to do with the fact that he didn't trust the media. Was Rich really dead? Nothing worse, in this case at least, than a pre-emptive death notice. Not that he was in any real doubt. Having said that, it might be an idea to drop round to Rich's office. Check it out for himself. He threw his jacket on, danced across the waxed oak floorboards and skipped out of the house, whistling merrily. Bach's *Come, Sweet Death*. The Bluegrass version.

He was approaching Intersects when his mobile rang. I noted, in passing, that there was a 'secret signing' on at lunchtime. I wouldn't have minded popping in to find out more. Too busy for that now, though, as Hayden had taken the call. Julius Okeke got straight to the point. 'You are *keen*, Hayden McGlynn,' he said.

'Sorry?'

'I refer to your erstwhile agent, Richard Mann: disposal of.'

'Thanks,' said Hayden. 'But all credit to Rich on that one.'

'Lucky then,' said Julius. 'Better still.'

And he was gone.

Hayden thought about what Julius had said. Maybe he *was* lucky. But there was now a disturbing undercurrent in his mental mix. What sort of man rejoices in the death of another? Assuming Rich was dead. He continued towards Camden on a troubled, nervous high.

\*

Richard Mann's Delancey Street office was on the first floor over a sign that read:

# Snip Snip
*Double vasectomies a specialty*
<small>We also cut hair</small>

Hayden stood on the edge of the pavement and stared up at Rich's window. No sign of – but there wouldn't be, would there? Unless – what if the media had got it wrong, and he was alive and well after all? No harm buzzing up; check Rich was one hundred per cent deceased. He was here now anyway. No harm buzzing up. He approached the door, thinking about what he'd say if Rich clicked him in. Tough one. Better all round if Rich was definitively dead.

His finger was on the buzzer when a man flew out of Snip Snip brandishing a pair of scissors with an agitated look in his eyes. He looked left, right and left again. He was about to retrace his steps when he noticed Hayden. 'I'm afraid he's –'

'I know,' said Hayden. 'Sad business. I've come to, you know...'

Difficult to find the right words. Fortunately, the hairdresser helped him out. 'Friend of Rich's, are we?'

'Client,' said Hayden. 'Well, ex-client.'

The hairdresser, more troubled now than agitated, was about to respond when he was interrupted by a loud cough from inside. 'Excuse *me*,' he said, possibly to the cough. He double clicked his scissors, turned to go in, then turned back to Hayden with what might have been a pleading look. 'Quick trim?'

Why not? thought Hayden. Quick trim. Maybe get the lowdown on Rich. The hairdresser probably knew everything there was to know. He was, after all, a hairdresser. So Hayden followed him in.

A man sat waiting in the hair chair, his huge, bulbous head sticking out from a black cape. 'Mark my words, Lindsey,' he said, 'the criminal fraternity will be up to no good while I sit here vegetating.'

Christ! A cop. Hayden sat down on a small wooden bench in an effort to disappear. 'Well, anyway,' said Lindsey, 'at least you've closed the book on poor Rich upstairs.' Christ! A cop on the Rich case!

The policeman did something with his face. Bit like a slow burn, but mischievous with it. 'Maybe I have,' he said, 'maybe I haven't.' He thought about this for a moment, then seemed to ripple at a private joke under the cape. 'Tell you what. How does this sound? Our friend upstairs was, by all accounts, a talent agent. Comedians and the like. Difficult little number that. I'm a big fan of the comedy genre, but you wouldn't get *me* up there.' He glanced over at Hayden, who sank further onto the bench. 'Stick to what you're good at, that's what *I* say.' A modest pause. 'DCI Pointer,' he said. 'Homicide.' Hayden was stunned into silence. Pointer? Wasn't he –? Hold on. *Top agent found dead. Detective Chief Inspector Ronnie Pointer, Camden Met, doesn't rule out accidental suicide.*

Pointer was off again. 'How about this as a hypothesis: you, Lindsey, had ambitions in that area. A budding young comedian in the making, cutting hair to pay the bills while he waits for his big break.' As Pointer continued, Lindsey snipped his comb-over nervously and made terrified eye contact with Hayden. 'You applied to the deceased for representation. His response? *As a comedian, pal, you'd make a great hairdresser.* Well, you weren't having that. Bloody nerve. So you sought revenge. Murder most foul.' He winked playfully at Hayden and prodded Lindsey from under the cape. 'Case closed?'

Lindsey looked as if he was about to burst into tears when he was suddenly distracted. An old couple out on the pavement had put a stepladder up inches from his window. 'I knew they'd be back,' he hissed, and, clutching his scissors with intent, he raced outside, yelling, 'Oi! Piddle off you infuriating old tossers!'

Pointer's head swivelled towards Hayden as the door slammed shut behind him. 'Bit of a backlog on the murder front at the mo, but I daresay we'll get round to it eventually. Thing is, he's not going anywhere. Bad business, though. Never met the departed myself, but as I say, big fan of the comedy genre. Young Paddy chap I have a particular liking for.' He chuckled at the memory. '*Termonfeckin. Yow!*'

He looked to Hayden for approval.

'Very...' said Hayden, 'very droll.'

Pointer nodded, beaming. Droll was good. He liked droll. 'So, what line of work are you in yourself, Pat?'

Hayden was wrong-footed. Pat? Oh, right. Pat. The accent. Hayden didn't want to get into a comedy conversation. Last thing he wanted was to be linked to Rich and, by implication,

Rich's death. 'Painter and decorator,' he lied. Bit of a cliché, but it worked.

'A worthy trade,' said Pointer. 'Got a business card?'

'Word of mouth,' improvised Hayden.

'That good, eh? Can't say I'm as successful myself. Not that I go touting for murder.'

He seemed to find something amusing in this as he studied Hayden's response. Hayden gave him his best rictus grin and glanced out the window. An agitated Lindsey was pointing furiously in the direction of elsewhere and the old couple hobbled off with their stepladder and a pot of paint, shamefaced. Lindsey then charged back in, scissors clicking furiously, eyes ablaze. 'Bloody anarchists. Two 'l's in specialty if you please. Some tosh about cultural colonisation. *I* don't know.' He glanced at the scissors, startled, stopped clicking and slid them 'discreetly' onto the counter. 'Anyway, Chief Inspector, all done. Let me get your coat.' He undid the cape and tittered nervously. 'Oh, and by the way, I really don't have any ambitions in that direction. No, I'd put Rich's death down to a tragic accident.' He turned to Hayden. 'I'm sure you'll back me up on this.'

Shit! Hayden was Painter and Decorator Pat to Pointer, ex-client of Rich to Lindsey. Pointer was waiting for a response. Hayden had to kill this before Lindsey grassed him up as someone with a potentially suspicious link to the deceased. 'Honest opinion?' he said. 'I say leave it to the experts.'

Pointer nodded his approval. 'Nice one, Pat. Nice one.' He set a couple of notes by the cash register, slipped his coat on, and gave Lindsey a quick shoulder squeeze. 'You do your job, mush, I'll do mine. Deal?' He turned to Hayden as he reached the door. He seemed to be sizing him up, which unnerved Hayden. Why would he do that? Was it a cop thing, or did he suspect something? 'Sure you didn't do it, Pat?' he said. 'You Irish, eh? Murder. It's in the blood.' He raised the hand of peace. 'Joke, Pat,' he said. 'Joke.'

And he was gone.

\*

As soon as Pointer had sauntered off, Lindsey locked the door, turned the sign to *Closed* and shut the blinds. He wrapped the cape around Hayden and, seemingly catatonic at this stage, pointed him to the hair chair. Hayden sat down, his brain on fire, and it wasn't that he'd put himself at the mercy of a neurotic time bomb with scissors. He'd killed his own father. He'd got away with it. He hadn't killed Richard Mann. What if he *didn't* get away with it? He had clear motive to kill Rich, after all, and something about Pointer put Hayden on edge. *Joke, Pat. Joke.* If it *was* a joke, it suggested Detective Chief Inspector Pointer was totally uninterested in Rich's death as murder. But what if it wasn't a joke? Could this be copper's bluff, cunning disguised as banter? If Pointer was on the case, it changed everything for *Bad Blood* and the script's new killer end – the *Rich Mann, Dead Mann* threat our hero makes to Rich's answerphone. Hayden would have to drop it. It was tantamount to an admission of guilt on the big screen! Hayden couldn't get rid of the feeling that he was sitting on the electric chair, with a psychotic hairdresser snipping away on his final earthly trim.

Snip snip. Snip snip snip. It should have been a soothing experience, the quick trim, but apart from the mounting paranoia, something else kept breaking into his thoughts. The sound of Lindsey snuffling. 'I was with him near the end,' he whimpered. 'I should never have left him alone.'

Hayden eyed Lindsey's reflection in the mirror. 'Sorry,' he said, 'but – you were *there*?'

There was something about the way Lindsey avoided eye contact. Bit shifty. As if he was hiding something. 'Not,' he replied, 'as such.'

Not as such? What the hell did that mean?

'Listen,' said Hayden, 'Rich was my friend.' He wasn't, but this was serious. 'Is there something you're not telling me here? I mean, you work directly below his office. Did you maybe hear noises?' Lindsey continued to snuffle but said nothing. 'Okay,

okay. Maybe not noises *as such.'* What about noises *not* as such? He felt like saying that but didn't.

Lindsey put the scissors down and blew his nose. 'Oh, Rich, Rich,' he said. 'Why? *Why*?!'

'Sorry,' said Hayden. 'But why what?'

Lindsey put his hands up to his head as if he was about to scream. 'He wasn't alone,' he wailed. 'Rich was not alone.'

At which point, in spite of Hayden's best efforts to get him to elaborate, Lindsey clammed up. Well, except to swear him to silence. As if Hayden had any intention of saying anything to anyone. But the fact that someone else had been there when Rich died – did that mean what Hayden thought it meant? That it *was* murder? How did Lindsey know that Rich hadn't been alone when he died, and why had he hidden this fact from Pointer?

Hayden was worried. It certainly hadn't been him who killed Rich, *he* knew that, but it would be a different matter trying to convince the cops, the judge, the jury. That's the way his mind was working. *Our hero – that's me, Rich – kills his agent. That's you, Rich. No idea how to do it yet, but don't worry. Hate will find a way.* He needed to change that ending! It was like a giant arrow pointing down at his head. Yes! It was me! I killed Rich! Hayden was already mentally tried, found guilty and banged up for life as Lindsey undid his cape and ushered him to the exit –

Straight into the arms of DCI Pointer. Bulky, intimidating Pointer, blocking the doorway. Huge hand on Hayden's petrified shoulder. 'You are well and truly nicked, my son,' he growled.

Hayden was about to have a heart attack when Lindsey appeared, clutching Pointer's gloves. 'The very thing,' said Pointer. 'Knew I'd forgotten something soon as I left. Couldn't figure out what it was. Fact is, I'd forget my doodah if it wasn't screwed on.' He pulled the gloves on and pinched Hayden's cheek. 'Had you there, Pat,' he smirked. 'I definitely had you there.'

# 9

I really felt for Hayden at this point but, as the omniscient narrator, I didn't feel the need to be with him as he made his hasty way back to his laptop to change the incriminating ending. He was going to go back, fiddle with a few scenes, agonise over the Marina sub-plot not reaching a joyful, life-enhancing climax, and ignore the accursed voiceover. Watching someone else's rewrite is hardly the stuff of classic drama, so I opted for a quick plot break courtesy of Intersects and the secret signing.

The bookshop was abuzz. Podium at the back. Signing table stacked up with the latest Melanie Schultz. Correction: Melanie 'Bud' Schultz. And no wonder it was billed as a secret signing. As *the* screenwriter's guru – I'm tempted to say The Screenwriters' Gurus' Screenwriter's Guru, but they probably all hate her – she could fill Wembley Stadium. Size-wise she's diminutive, reputation-wise she's huge.

*Write Bucks!!!*
*The New Write!!!*

Both bestselling how-to books. I could go on – she's written dozens – but pride of place went to the about-to-be-published *They Seek Him There,* her long-awaited sequel to *They Seek Him Here: The Chameleon Life of Wolfe Swift.*

Her voice boomed from the back of the room. I hadn't spotted her behind the podium. I'm tempted to write her speech in block capitals, 36 font, Braggadocio Bold. But I won't.

# NO GIMMICKS

'Okay. Call me Bud. You've read my books. They've changed your life. That's why you're here. Okay two. Three rules for successful screenwriting. Never use one small word where none will do. If you introduce a beautiful woman in scene one, the lead gets to fuck her at the end.' A sharp intake of breath here from several audience members. 'Brutally murdered is also good.' Collective intake of breath. This was inflammatory stuff. 'Last rule. Get Wolfe Swift. It's not a screenwriting rule, but Wolfe Swift breaks all rules. Questions!'

A male hand shot straight up. Relax, he was speaking on behalf of the feminists. 'What if the lead is a woman?'

'She can go fuck her*self*.'

A short pause as the audience processed this. One of the bookshop staff took the opportunity, in the brief lull, to stagger a set of bookshelf steps across the room and place them behind the podium. A short pause and lo! Bud appeared. Still diminutive, but visible. Average head. Miniscule everything else. 'Next!'

Different voice. 'Who would you get to play you in a biopic?'

'Wolfe Swift.'

'But he's a man.'

Melanie 'Bud' seethed. Her micro-hands grabbed the side of the podium and almost squeezed the life out of it. Her head throbbed in violent sympathy. 'Are you saying I can't be a man because I'm a woman? Can't be black because I'm white? Can't be French because I'm from the Bronx? Can't be a globe artichoke because I'm a fucking *person*? Where have you *been*, lady? That was then. This is now. Let the dead bury their dead. Don't define me with words, woman. Don't box me in, bitch.'

'But – but I'm a man.'

'Oh.' Long pause. 'Really?' The first hesitation from Bud. The merest hint, perhaps, of vulnerability.

A woman – I think, I'm all confused now – came to her rescue. 'The Oscars. Any favourite for best film?'

Bud was back on top. '*Invisible Woman.* No question.'

An audible, and collective, sigh of disappointment. Very obvious answer. You'd expect something a bit more quotable from this demolisher of shibboleths, this iconoclast, this tiny Amazon. But *Invisible Woman*? It was everyone's favourite. No controversy there. What was Bud thinking? You'd expect something *beyond* controversial in her case. Some film not even on the list. One that hadn't been made yet. But no. *Invizz*, as it was commonly called, got her vote. 200 years in the life of a black woman written out of American history. I won't spoil it for you by outlining the plot, but it's heartbreaking and uplifting in equal measure, with a luminous central performance, all the more stunning because she stays literally invisible throughout yet burns a hole through the screen with the sheer intensity of her acting. And here's the other extraordinary thing. The actress chose to remain anonymous – unheard of in the history of Hollywood. She might change her mind, however, if she won the Oscar. Back to Bud. 'Plus, I got me a hunch on best actress.'

She paused for dramatic effect. No response from the audience. The manager raised an embarrassed hand. 'Who?'

The answer, again, was pretty obvious. Sherilee Lewis. She too was everyone's favourite, so no surprises there. Not that Bud had named her yet, but she would. Sorry, he would. Sorry, he/she/they/it would. Hold on. Let's stick to she, for this draft anyway. *She* would. The audience, as one self-identifying unit, fully expected it. Bit of a damp squib as far they were concerned. Not that Bud seemed to notice. 'Wait for it.' She paused again for extra dramatic effect. Opened an imaginary envelope. Took the imaginary contents out. 'And the winner is –' she glanced at the imaginary sheet. 'Wow.' A look of mock disbelief. She glanced at the sheet again. 'Wolfe Swift!'

The room froze, and so did everyone in it. Not least the bookshop manager. Was this really happening? Melanie 'Bud' Schultz, predicting a *white man* playing a *black woman*? Sorry again. A Caucasian male playing a woman of colour? In his shop? This was – this was highly contentious. This was *sacrilege*. A voice broke the silence from the floor. Man? Woman? Black? White? Other? I'm not getting involved. 'But...' it blurted. 'But...'

Bud craned her neck over the podium and stubbed a finger at the shocked faces staring up from the floor. 'Fuck *but*! Mr Wolfe Swift, the finest actress of his generation, has already won six Oscars. He never turns up to collect. If he doesn't turn up this time, you'll know old Bud was right.'

*

Now that was some moment. I mean, talk about trying to sell your book. Total nonsense to any sane person, but by the time I left the bookshop it had probably circumnavigated the globe twice. File under crackpot theories. But what energy! Bud was certainly a zeitgeisty kinda gal, and, if I may be permitted to digress for a moment, I found her curiously inspirational. I may have mentioned my own scriptwriting in passing. Haven't had a great deal of success so far and while I may not be in the first flush of youth, wasn't Han Sung Yee 112 when he had his first and only haiku published after a life of meditation?[9] My point? I wasn't finished yet. Unproduced projects littered my past. Wonderful ideas. Trust me. Example: *Ravishing*. Glamorous Dublin woman on strict beauty diet gets transported back to

---

[9] It wasn't very good, but that's beside the point.

famine era Ireland. I don't want to give the plot away, but her constant refrain, 'God, I'm absolutely *ravishing*,' supplied the title to what I can only describe as a vicious satire on contemporary mores.

No backers. 'For fuck's sake, Macker, the punters'd string us up.' Typical response from the film world of the time. And speaking of time, I was often referred to, in comedy circles, as being ahead of mine. Well, it was said once, but I repeated it often, and being ahead of your time can lead to a lifetime of almost. Take the case of American stand-up Mort de'Ath, who called his unpublished autobiography *Seventeen Minutes*. Mort was ahead of his time. Seventeen minutes ahead. Always seventeen. But time, in life at least, never caught up. He died a broken man. Seventeen minutes later? Book deal.

Maybe, just maybe, the same applied to me, but the big difference is that Mort was dead, I wasn't, and Melanie 'Bud' Shultz had inspired me. More, she'd filled me with hope and longing but this, as I've probably said before, is not about me. Back to the plot or, put it another way, Hayden. He'd have finished his minor-adjustment rewrite by now and was, no doubt, having a celebratory pot of Assam, prior to whacking the finished product off to Wolfe.

\*

He wasn't, because nothing in World of Hayden is ever quite that simple. He hadn't even begun his rewrite. Instead, he was pacing up and down the open-plan floor beneath the magnificent steel and glass staircase, in a state of no small agitation. And who can blame him? Sitting at his desk, poring over Hayden's laptop in a seeming trance, Wolfe Swift, unexpectedly back from Dublin, was almost literally devouring the script.

Such intensity. From both of them, come to think of it. Wolfe lost in the story, the odd *mnn* or *nnng* or *tsk* the only signs of approval or otherwise. Hayden desperately craving praise. Big moment for him. Difficult to know which way it would go,

Wolfe's control of his facial muscles and enigmatic eyes being something to behold, although Hayden didn't get to see those bits.

I've often wondered what drives a man like Wolfe Swift. Such poise, such surface equanimity. Yet he spends most of his life inhabiting other people. Why? Most great artists carry a wound that drives them on. Was this the case with Swift? Because it certainly didn't look like it; on the surface at least. He was dressed in what can best be described as casual chic. Crushed silk/linen-mix suit by Luigi Popparelli. Silk pencil scarf with matching socks, both Claudia Dapper. Doe-hide loafers by Gladys McGee. Must have cost a fortune but, crucially, didn't look it. I mention his sartoriality because it seemed to want to be mentioned. Everything about Wolfe Swift wanted to be mentioned. He couldn't help it. He oozed charisma. Even the eyes, relaxed now that he wasn't in character, were burning into the script.

He sat there for a seeming eternity, lost in the deep intensity of his thoughts. He straightened up, closed the laptop and pressed his slim, feminine-yet-masculine fingers to his temple. Hayden stopped pacing. This was the moment. All that work. Was it a yes or was it a no? Wolfe could make him or Wolfe could break him. Which was it to be? Wolfe flicked a graceful foot against the polished oak floorboards and twirled round on the typing chair to face Hayden. 'Good,' he said. 'Pretty damn good.' Hayden whooped inwardly and danced a ridiculous jig. On the outside he nodded his head. A kind of shrug-nod. A helluva-lot-of-work-but-hey nod. Humility and chutzpah. Wolfe pushed his chair back. 'Couple of points. We can kill the voiceover. Love the three aunts. Touch of Greek mythology there? More, please. Oh, and a quick word about the end.'

'Ah,' said Hayden, 'I wanted to speak to you about that.' Wolfe did the you-have-the-floor thing with his hand. 'Fact is,' said Hayden, 'I've sort of rewritten the ending in my head. The agent, see, is a minor character. Probably not a great idea to involve him in the ending. Keep the camera on the story, right? So cut the agent, stick with the main man. It should end with me, him that is, writing the, you know, the script.' He'd pretty well trailed off at this point. It sounded a bit limp. As did this bit. 'An in-the-end-is-the-beginning type thing, you know?'

Wolfe waved all this away with a dismissive hand. 'Not what I had in mind,' he said. 'Killer end. Love it. But he's got to be in bed with Marina when he makes the death threat call. Sex and death. Explosive.'

Hayden was totally thrown. In bed with Marina? What was Wolfe Swift's motivation here? Where was he going with this? But wind back a bit. Julius Okeke's office. Hayden overcome with a wave of unbidden emotion at the mention of Marina's name. Marina lived across the road from Eddie's house in Dublin. Hayden had thought she was a prostitute. She wasn't. She'd been good to Eddie, and Hayden, with her apparent calling in mind, had misread good. But good, in this case, simply meant good. With Hayden, though, she'd been playful – possibly more than playful. Flirtatious?

And now Wolfe's suggestion. Hayden wasn't happy about it. Worse. He was very, very *un*happy. 'But – but I wasn't in bed with Marina.' He almost spluttered this.

Wolfe shrugged. 'A detail.'

'Sorry, I thought you wanted me to write what really happened.'

'Fair enough up to a point,' said Wolfe. 'But only up to a point. Artistic license. You know?'

I knew. Hayden didn't. Interesting, however, that in certain respects Wolfe Swift, The Greatest Actor Of This Or Any Other Age, modern male incarnate, was unreconstructed old school. Hayden, however, had nowhere left to go. 'Okay,' he said. 'I can fix the Marina angle.'

'You do that. Give the punters something they can hang onto. Maybe she –'

'Okay, okay,' said Hayden. He wasn't exactly thrilled about Wolfe bursting in on his bedroom fantasy. Which is exactly what it was. Him. Marina. Soft lights. And strictly no third-party involvement. Particularly Wolfe. There was something beyond disturbing about that. 'Leave it with me,' he said. 'Consider it done.'

Wolfe nodded his approval. 'And the voiceover. Wolfe Swift is begging you. Fix the fucking voiceover.'

'Trust me,' said Hayden. 'It's gone. But the phone call from the agent. Let's drop it, okay?'

'Sex and death,' said Wolfe. 'No phone call, no death. Sex and –. Doesn't work, see?'

Joke? Hard to tell. No clue from the mesmerising stare.

'Nice one,' said Hayden. 'It's just – well, it's a bit complicated.'

'Life is complicated,' said Wolfe. 'That's what makes it so beautiful.'

Moot point. Hayden tried again. 'Thing is, the guy it's based on, my ex-agent, is, well – he died.'

'Brilliant,' said Wolfe. He thought about this for a moment. 'You didn't kill him, did you?'

'Course not,' said Hayden.

'Well then. That's your dedication right there.' Wolfe leapt out of the chair and rubbed his hands together. 'This is beginning to feel very, very real.'

# 10

Amazing how quickly you can get rid of voiceover from a film script when you put your mind to it. Cut cut cut. Gone. It brought up several other issues that Hayden dealt with over the next few days, which left him at the final section. He, Hayden, leaves the Nautical Buoy, arrives back at Eddie's, looks longingly over at Marina's house. A red coupé flies along the road, open-top, Marina smiling as she catches sight of the object of her desire. Cut to Marina's double bed. The blankets tossed pre-, inter-, then post-coitally. Hayden's mobile rings. He takes the call as Marina snuggles up. Rich on the line being Rich. Hayden threatens to kill him. Marina, Rich. Sex and death. *No idea how to do it yet, but don't worry. Hate will find a way.* Credits. And yes, Wolfe Swift was right. Cinematically, it was perfect.

You'd be forgiven for thinking that this ending was as good as a signed confession of guilt for the murder of Richard Mann. So why had Hayden written it? Call it divine inspiration because, once he started, all negative thoughts disappeared and out it flowed. A God-wrote-it-I-merely-held-the-quill moment, if he wanted to be modest about it. Taking the call in bed with Marina felt *right*, as Wolfe had suggested it would. It was also total fiction, unlike the rest of the script, but writing it had affected Hayden in an alpha male sort of way. He felt like the dashing hero in an Edith Wimple novel. Not that he'd read any of her massive output,[10] but he knew the type. Dark, brooding,

---

[10] *Still Beats My Heart. And Not To Yield.* I could go on.

masterful. This ego self-massage totally eclipsed any thoughts of what the repercussions might be if the death of Richard Mann became a murder enquiry. He was about to wallow in an erotic reverie when his mobile went. His three Dublin aunts. End of reverie.

'Howaya, Hayding. We were wondering if you were dead yet.'
'Obviously not, or you wouldn't have come to the phone.'
'Not that you come to a mobile as such, Hayding.'
'Being as what it's already there. Hence the word mobile.'
Ping. The word 'mobile' registered with Hayden. Subliminally. But the aunts chattered merrily on.
'So anyway, how's tings?'
'That's Rusty barking in the background, by the way.'
'He misses you someting terrible.'
'Oh, and by the way, we seen the lovely Marina down Madden's this very a.m.'
'She seemed oddly distrait, if you follow.'
'Almost as if she was nursing some secret sorrow.'
'Pining for a lost love, poot être?'
'Do we make ourselves clear, Hayding?'
'You could do a lot worse.'
The three aunts seemed happy to continue the conversation uninterrupted, so Hayden put the mobile down on the desk and twirled his chair around on its swiveller. Which meant he missed the next bit: 'And by the way, she only went and asked for your number!'

*

The chair swivel. Dramatic moment. It placed him at eye level with Wolfe Swift's black-jeaned legs. Wolfe was standing halfway up the stairs, immobile, and he seemed to have undergone a subtle, almost imperceptible, change. As if he was somehow elsewhere. Except he wasn't. He was staring intently at Hayden through rapacious, wolfish eyes. It felt as if Hayden had disappeared into them and been subsumed whole. He wanted to check in a mirror to see if he was still there. But he didn't. What if he wasn't? That's how disconcerting it was.

All pretty riveting stuff from Wolfe. How did he do it? Equally interesting from a psychological viewpoint, *why* did he do it? What drove him to study his subject with such intensity, then disappear totally as himself; to spend well over half his life literally *being* other people? I had no way of knowing. In fact, I doubt very much whether he could answer the question himself. Fascinating to see him try, though. Not now, however, because now he wasn't himself. He was – Hayden? Not there yet, perhaps, but those jeans – very Haydenesque. Black. Mass market. No more casual chic. Wolfe Swift's legs were Hayden to the life.

In an effort to snap out of this seeming daymare, Hayden fell back on a tradition passed down from generation to generation in times of crisis by his English relatives. He put the kettle on. When he finally steeled himself and turned back to the stairs, Wolfe had disappeared. The aunts, however, were still there. He'd forgotten all about them, but tiny voices coming from the desk drew him back to his mobile. He picked it up. The tiny voices got slightly less tiny.

'I don't know if anyone else has noticed, ladies, but Hayding hasn't said a word.'

'Do you tink maybe he *is* dead?'

'A sad day indeed if so. His like will not be here again.'

'Requiescat in pace, Hayding.'

'And flights of angels sing dee to dy rest!'

Hayden wasn't dead, but if certain things came to pass he'd be as good as.

The ping had slowly registered.

The subliminal had risen to the surface, and with it paranoia.

A film script was one thing – that was fiction.

But an answerphone message from Hayden including a death threat to Richard Mann?

That – no question – was fact.

## 11

No crime scene tape on the door, but Hayden could almost feel Pointer's oversized cop hand on his shoulder as he pressed the entry code to Rich's office. *One two three four, Ay. Who's going to think of that?* Rich Mann's little joke.

Click.

'Anyone home?' he shouted, his voice echoing in the empty stairwell. Then, to be on the safe side, 'Rich?'

No answer. He ran his dry tongue across his dry lips and took the stairs two at a time. Get it over with. He pulled his jacket sleeve down over his hand and opened the glass door. The place seemed eerily calm. Understandable really. It usually had Rich in it, with his feet on the desk, ruining someone's career. Now, however, it was empty.

A quick trawl of the desktop. Nothing. Hayden was about to check the drawers when he saw that the door behind the desk was ajar. In all the times he'd visited, he'd never seen that door open. Not once. He went over and eased it further open with his foot. A bedroom! Of sorts. A bed. Probably not meant for sleeping in. Centre stage, a sexual fetish apparatus – straps, chains, body-harness, ankle and wrist limb-cuffs – dangled from the ceiling. On the floor, a discarded *Sex Toys R Us* box, a bullwhip coiled up like a dead cobra and, protruding from the bed, a Victorian peeler's truncheon. An altar-like table with half-burned silver and black candles and a bowl of wizened tangerines. The faint, and slightly incongruous, smell of incense. *Detective Chief Inspector Ronnie Pointer refuses to comment further but doesn't rule out accidental suicide.* That about summed it up. Rich spent his workdays abusing others, he relaxed by abusing himself. No sign of any police activity, so Pointer must have gone for the suicide option. Hayden turned back to the office and retraced his steps to the desk.

Top drawer, right hand. Sure enough, there it was. Rich's mobile, with Hayden's answerphone death threat, was sitting on a thick sheaf of contracts. Rich, Hayden noted with approval, was a fastidious creature of habit. Work late. Tidy up. Fuck self. Well, slight change of plan at the end there – for 'fuck', read 'top' – but no harm in that. We all need to break out of our comfort zone sometimes.

Hayden slipped the mobile into his jacket pocket and leafed through the contracts. Interesting. Comedians all, and Hayden had worked with every single one. Les Mahagoe. Darley Sweeting. Lenny Broonstein. Stand-ups too numerous to mention. Any one of them possibly guilty of this most heinous of crimes – if that's truly what it was. He removed his own contract and put the others tidily back. They'd keep the crime squad busy with people who weren't him. As he closed the drawer he felt the tension ease.

'Hello?'

The voice – Pointer?! Second thoughts about suicide?! – floated up from the foot of the stairs. Hayden looked around in panic, scrunched the contract into his pocket, crossed to the window, undid the latch, pulled it silently up. Outside the window – oh, serendipity! – an ancient, rusting, fire escape. He clambered out, gingerly closed the window and fled down the metal steps.

\*

Heart pounding, Hayden made his way along a back alley past a row of bins till he was out on the street. He strolled, sham-relaxed, past Snip Snip. He could see Lindsey at the foot of Rich's stairs, a puzzled look on the back of his upturned head. Hayden walked quickly past, along the street, left onto

Kentish Town Road and homeward. He tore his contract into strips and deposited them in a succession of recycling bins en route. Nothing unethical there either. *It's a till death do us part type thing, Ay.* Well, they'd come to the part bit. Rich was dead. The contract was null and void. The strips of paper were simply that. Strips of null and void. He'd reached the place where the road passes over Regent's Canal when he finally felt safe enough to prise Rich's mobile from his pocket. The one with the answerphone message from Hayden. *He kills his agent. That's you, Rich.* Probably a good idea to chuck it in the canal and dispose of it forever. But what if someone saw him and thought it looked suspicious? Which it was.

Worse, what if –

What if, what if, what if? Best, all round, to chuck the bloody thing in the water and stride on. He had enough to think about with the script. So Hayden, for once, acted on impulse. He chucked the bloody thing in. He strode on.

But here's the interesting bit. The second, truncated what if. What if a barge was travelling underneath, and the mobile fell on the barge, the barge pilot, a woman of unimpeachable honesty, dropped it into the local police station, the police had a quick look to establish ownership, discovered Hayden's message, thought *Interesting, could be one for the murder squad*, and passed it on to Pointer?

Bit far-fetched? Perhaps. Besides, Hayden's thoughts, once he'd got rid of the mobile, were concentrated elsewhere. As far as he was concerned, the mobile was out of the picture.

# 12

Hayden woke the following morning, head buried deep in his goose down pillow, to the sound of birdsong. Sweet, innocent birdsong. He got up, pulled on his jeans – black, always black – and headed for the stairs. Halfway down, he stopped. Wolfe Swift lay across the sofa, sneering at the ceiling, spitting into his mobile. 'While we're on the subject, *Rich*, my name is Hayden. Two syllables, with a H.' Pause. 'He'll be supporting himself, Rich. Can't do it. I'm dealing with a bereavement at the moment. And I'm writing a novel, actually.' Another pause. 'Early days yet, but –' Hayden sat on the stairs and stared through the bannisters, spellbound. This was him. Hayden McGlynn. Verbatim. 'Much as I'd like to chat all night, *Dickie*, I've decided I'd prefer, on balance, to sit alone in a darkened room and decompose.'

A three-second pause, which seemed a lot longer. Wolfe was making you feel the pain. The genius of screen acting isn't acting, it's reacting, and Wolfe was a master. The camera loved him, even when it wasn't there. When it wasn't there it pined for him, and it was pining now. Hayden stayed where he was, still spellbound. Spellbound and hugging the bannister.

Wolfe rose wearily from the sofa and went over to the kitchen. He put the kettle on. Hayden was gasping for a hot drink himself, but he had no intention of joining Wolfe in the beverage-making ritual and besides, he was hypnotised by Wolfe's body language. Languid with the odd nervy little jerk. An absent-minded hand up the t-shirt for a quick scratch. He even rearranged his crotch at one point, which Hayden found a bit off-putting. He wouldn't do that if someone was watching him. Except he would, because Wolfe's crotch rearrangement was quintessential McGlynn. Hayden did it unconsciously and, therefore, unselfconsciously. Not often but, in the case of crotch rearrangement, even once is once too often.

The kettle prepared to boil. Wolfe removed the filter from the teapot. He tapped the used tea leaves into the recycling bin, replaced the teapot filter and poured in a couple of inches of the now boiled water. Swirled it round, emptied it into a cup, placed the pot on a tray, took the lid off the caddy and measured two heaped teaspoons of finest Assam into the filter. Boiling water on top, lid on, cosy on teapot, four-minute wait. Perfect. Well, almost. Three heaped teaspoons, always three, but it was early days; perfection could wait. Or, and this might be the view of some critics au fait with the tea-making process: the character was imperfect, Wolfe wasn't. There was perfection in his imperfection.

Three point five minutes. Wolfe opened the fridge, took out the milk, removed the plastic lid, poured the water from the heated cup into the sink and emptied the remains of the milk into the cup. Damn! He finished the milk. Hayden would have to do without his early morning brew till he'd abluted and gone to the shops!

Wolfe was about to take his first sup when a text pinged in. He glanced at his mobile.

'Shit!'

This, whatever it was, was serious. He put the cup down on the worktop, went over to the writing desk and opened Hayden's laptop. Went online. Typed something into the search bar. Stared at the screen. Scrolled down, muttering furiously to himself. He stood up, charged across the floor and, totally oblivious to Hayden hugging the bannister, took the stairs three steps at a time. This was great acting. So great, in fact, that it probably wasn't acting. Ah. That explained it. He'd obviously come out of character. Interesting. Total immersion would presumably come later. Hayden waited till he'd disappeared, then went to see what he'd left onscreen.

*Wolfe Swift Outed as Invisible Woman by Mad Mel!*

He scrolled down and speed-read the article. Patently a pile of tosh which took Melanie 'Bud' Schultz's blatant self-publicity in the bookshop at face value, but these days people will believe anything.

*

Milk. Hayden had popped out to buy it when his mobile went. Julius Okeke's voice rang in his ear. 'Hayden McGlynn. You have worked hard. The script is ready. Wolfe Swift is happy with his new ending. Julius Okeke is therefore happy. You will sign a contract. You will submit your bank details. From these simple but necessary acts, good things will happen. But now is the time to move on. Permit me to illustrate this with a story. When I was growing up in Botswana we lived in a small village. There was one goat for the whole village. Every morning my father would say, *My first and most precious son, when I am gone, do not forget to feed the beast.* That is what we called it. The beast. My father went to study accountancy in the big city. At least, that is what he told us he was doing. To my shame I neglected to feed the beast. The beast died, and that is why I say to you, Hayden McGlynn, do not forget to feed the beast or the beast will assuredly die. Do I make myself clear?'

'You want another script,' said Hayden.

'That is what I want,' said Julius Okeke. 'That is precisely what I want. I want it on my desk. I want it now.' And he was gone.

# 13

The pace has been pretty frenetic up to now. Mercifully, though, the mood is about to soften, and Hayden to show the sweeter side of his nature for once. It's been buried deep, to be blunt, but that's what murder, paranoia and naked ambition can do to a man. And those addicted to the whodunit might be a bit miffed that we've taken our eye off the corpse. All in good time. Hayden has had a lot on his mind.

Writing is a strange business. It can be an excavation of the subconscious, uncovering truths otherwise left buried. I'm referring, here, to Hayden's script. What did it tell him about himself? He seemed unable to think or talk about Marina without getting choked up, but experienced pure pleasure in writing himself into a bedroom scene with her. He'd left Ireland without contacting her. Big mistake. Marina had given him her business card. He kept it in his wallet. Next to his heart if we're going to be romantic about it. But that might have been mere coincidence: it's where the breast pocket is situated. He whipped it out. He'd email her work address, which doesn't sound very romantic. Work email? The very term seems to dictate both style and content. And so it proved. In the initial act of composition he kept thinking about Marina's offer of a double session and couldn't help returning, in his head, to the world of psychotherapy. With specific reference to the fact, not that he'd killed his father, but that he had three mothers. Inference? He possibly did need help. This, in turn, led him to start the letter *Dear Ms Courtney*.

He was about to give up at *Dear Ms Courtney, Further to our recent meeting, and with specific reference to your kind offer of a double session,* when he spotted something on the writing desk which was about to change his whole modus operandi. A tray of writing paper. Beautiful, top of the range, grainy vellum. Matching lilac envelopes. Modern methods of communication are so impersonal, clinical even, but the beautifully composed love letter on best quality paper? Nonpareil. The very smell of it made Hayden think in French. *Dear Ms Courtney?* Bin! Try again. *Chère Marina.* That was about as far as his French went, but it was enough. His innermost thoughts flew out. Several times. The first version had a couple of typos and a passage so top-heavy with subordinate clauses that he couldn't reread it. If he couldn't she wouldn't, so he toned it down with matching tippex. The finished missive was rich with suppressed longing and over-ripe metaphor, but thankfully adverb-free.[11] He folded it neatly, slipped it into the envelope, licked the flap lovingly and sealed it before he changed his mind. Or decided on yet another rewrite.

Although, on second thoughts…

No. That was it. He'd literally sealed his fate. For better or worse. Time, now, for a quick shower. I didn't follow him in there. Nudity? It's not that sort of book. But what if Hayden slipped and cracked his skull? Should I not, at least, keep an eye on developments? So I did.

Hayden was in the bathroom. Shower cubicle. Frosted glass door. All very discreet. I left him to it. Minutes later, and this is what I couldn't understand at first, he was off out the front door. Unbelievable. I've heard of a quick douche, but there he was, dry, fully dressed, gone. But hold on. I could still hear the shower. One of those power jobs that resonates through brick. So, how could he still be in the shower and – you'll be well

---

[11] See *The Annotated Hewbris* (pp 641-8) for full reproduction of all twelve drafts. With special scented-vellum scratch 'n' sniff feature on the hardback's inside cover.

ahead of me here. The Hayden who left the house was in fact The Greatest Actor Of This Or Any Other Age, Wolfe Swift, preparing for his next big role. Chameleonic genius or what?! He had *me* fooled, and I'm the author!

Identity established, I was out the door fast, because Wolfe as Hayden was no slouch. He made his way down Kentish Town Road, no detours, straight to Intersects. In the door, up to the counter of Browse & Quaff, he ordered two lattes – two! – grabbed a table, sat down and glanced at his watch. Moments later, the door swung open and in swung Bo Bell. She looked around, his hand went up in greeting, she went over.

'Perfect timing,' he said. He pointed at the coffee. 'Hope I got that right.'

'Black,' said Bo, 'always black. But what the hell.' She sat down and lifted the latte in a toast. 'This coffee is happy to self-identify.' Weird though, she thought. She'd had coffee with him here just days ago. Double espresso. Difficult to see a latte when you looked at a double-e. Speaking of which. 'You took Aunty Bo's advice, I see.'

'Advice?' Wolfe almost pierced her with his eyes. Not Hayden eyes. Wolfe eyes. 'Sorry, what advice?'

Bo looked a bit taken aback. 'No sugar,' she said. 'Remember? Sugar? Teeth?'

Wolfe moved forward in his seat. 'No. Sorry again. What about sugar? And teeth?'

'You know,' said Bo. 'The thing you were doing last time with the sugar bowl. Bit, I don't know... Look, forget it. You were on edge.'

'No,' said Wolfe. 'Tell me. I need to know.'

Bo was worried now. 'Are you okay, Hayden? I mean, you've been under a lot of pressure lately, right? Maybe we should –'

'Hayden' leaned over and squeezed her hand. She winced.

'Sorry,' he said. 'Bit tense. But show me. Please.'

Bo sighed, stood up and went to the counter. She grabbed a sugar bowl from a tray and came back. 'Okay,' she said. '*I'm* talking to *you*. Coffee down, coffee up. Quick sip, coffee back down. That's the way it's usually done, right? You, on the other hand. Watch.' She didn't need to say it. Those eyes. Those lupine eyes. 'Coffee down, coffee still down. Sugar lump up.'

She chose a brown sugar lump from the bowl and held it between her thumb and middle finger. Wolfe nodded in concentration. 'Brown, right?' he said.

'Well,' said Bo, 'it's not exactly something I've studied in detail. I do have a life outside, but that's what you usually do. Yes.'

'Okay,' said Wolfe. 'Brown up. Got you. What then?'

'Are you sure you're all right?' said Bo. 'You do know you can get help.'

Wolfe didn't seem to hear. 'So, I'm holding the brown sugar lump in my – what? – my left hand?'

'Left hand,' said Bo. 'Always left. You roll it like a dice.' Wolfe is about to ask how many times. Bo knows this. Something about the look. 'Six times. Exactly six. You crumble it into the cup. Stir like so. Then –'

'Yes!?' A bit too loud, but Wolfe knew that. He lowered his voice. 'Sorry. Yes?'

'Same thing with a white lump. But no rolling with this one. Just crumble. Into the saucer. Not the cup this time. The saucer.'

'Thanks,' said Wolfe. 'That's – that's very helpful.'

Bo gave him a look. A what-is-this-man-on look. 'Brown, roll, crumble,' she said. 'White, just crumble. Then it's one for each hand. Brown left, white right. Got that?'

Wolfe nodded, still deep in concentration. Brown roll crumble, white just crumble. Brown left, white right. Repeat. Brown roll crumble, white just crumble. Brown left, white right. Bo watched, mesmerised. Fourth time round –

'Okay,' she said. 'Busy day.' No response. She pushed her untouched latte away and stood up. 'In that case,' she said, 'glad to be of service.'

But Wolfe was lost in world of sugar lumps. Staring at the bowl as if it might disappear. As Bo left the shop, he chose a brown one, held it delicately between thumb and middle finger, and started to roll it, meditatively, like a dice.

*

If you've read *Sloot* you'll be aware that I once lost Hayden, literally, in pursuit of my comedy guru, Professor Emeritus Stern.[12] Lose Hayden and you lose the plot, because Hayden, in a sense, *is* the plot. I left Wolfe to his sugar lumps and followed in Bo's wake back up the Kentish Town Road, back towards Wolfe's and, I hoped, Hayden. He'd have finished his shower by now, so where would he be? Still in the general vicinity if I was lucky. But what if he wasn't? I had no three aunts to help me out this time. However, I needn't have worried. Bo, en route to wherever she was going herself, did a double take. She'd spotted Hayden up ahead, standing beside a post-box, staring at his mobile. Impossible, surely, but it certainly seemed to be Hayden. Bo's thoughts: How could it possibly be? She'd left him grinding sugar lumps half a mile back.

It was, in fact, eminently possible. That was Wolfe Hayden, this was Hayden Hayden. Staring, as I say, at his mobile. A text had pinged in.

> *Hi. Got yr number from three aunts. In London for conference at KCH. Last minute but love to meet for drink there @ 9 if poss? If not – soon? Marina x*

Hayden was ecstatic. *x?!!!* He'd posted the letter to Marina, and now this. As if she'd anticipated the letter and read his mind.

He checked the time. Marina was right about last minute. It was 8.12. KCH. He knew it. Keynote Conference Hotel, Knightsbridge. Should be on time if he headed over now. He

---

[12] *'With hilarious consequences'* – the Catholic Herald, the Jerusalem Post *and* Marxism Today

texted back. *On way.* He toyed with *x* but decided, on balance, against. Marina's *x* suggested intimacy. His might be read as needy.

'Hayden?'

Bo had reached the post-box, still confused. Hayden looked up from his mobile. 'Bo. Love to chat but –' he waved the mobile by way of explanation '– gotta dash. Coffee soon? My shout.' And he was off.

Bo stared after him as he went. Then she shrugged, the what-can-you-do shrug, and continued on her way.

Hayden felt like the hero of a romantic comedy as he headed for Kentish Town tube. The race to the airport scene. Not that Marina was flying off anywhere. She'd still be there at 9.03, for instance. But love spurred Hayden on, and the fates were on his side. Kentish Town to Leicester Square. 8.27. Bang on time.

Hayden was standing on the Piccadilly Line platform at Leicester Square, waiting for a connection, when it happened. The tube pulled in. The crowd bustled forward. Hayden positioned himself. The tube doors opened. Two doors down, out came Julius Okeke followed by an incandescent Melanie 'Bud' Schultz. As they prised their way through the crowd, Bud poked Julius in the lower back with a furious finger.

'It is not a race issue, amigo,' she roared. 'It is a Wolfe Swift issue!'

Julius Okeke stopped and turned to face her. His voice was lower and more measured than hers. Beautifully modulated. 'I very much doubt that on biological grounds, my esteemed friend,' he said.

Hayden prised his way onto the carriage.

'Permit me to illustrate my thesis with a little story,' continued Julius. 'When I was growing up in –'

The double doors were closing. I was faced with a choice, but really there was no choice. I hopped on the tube with Hayden, so I missed a potentially riveting altercation. As the tube pulled away I saw Bud whack Julius over the head with a copy of her

Wolfe book, but I'd made the right decision. The big love scene? I couldn't afford to miss it.

>Leicester Square to Hyde Park Corner. 8.46.

>8.52 as Hayden emerged and raced along Knightsbridge.

>9.03. Arrival at destination.

So, bit of a damp squib on the romcom front.

*

The Keynote Conference Hotel glowed in front of Hayden. All glass front and attitude. He peered in as he made his way to the entrance. A long, narrow, brightly lit bar traversed the ground floor. High ceiling, black tables, white leather seats, flickering candles, lots of empty space. Very classy. Then, through the window, he spotter her: alone at a table, head buried deep in a work folder, sat Marina.

Marina.

How often had he almost bought her flowers when he was still in Dublin? How often had he almost knocked on her door? What had stopped him? She'd promised him a double session. But Marina was a psychotherapist. What if she thought he was nuts? Mentally challenged? Whatever the term, Hayden hadn't knocked on her door and swept her, metaphorically, into his manly arms. Because Hayden, in matters of the heart, was a ditherer. Besides, he possibly *was* nuts.

He awoke as if from a dream. Marina was waving at him. And smiling. Hayden felt a heart-surge, a wave of pure elation, as he went inside. Glass door to the foyer, glass door to the bar. Marina, still smiling, rose to meet him. He stood facing her, unsure what to do next.

'I've ordered for both of us,' said Marina. 'Hope that's okay.' Hayden glanced at the table. A spritzer and a bottle of lager. One on each side. She squeezed his hand. 'Relax. I checked your dietary requirements. It's alcohol-free.'

He sat down as if in a dream. She smiled at him across the table, and he felt as if he was falling into her beautiful, dark brown eyes. That perfect, once-in-a-lifetime moment. He was about to raise the bottle to his lips when –

'Oh, our *gosh*! It's Marina *Court*ney! Mind if we squeeze *in* here?'

'We are such great *fans* of your –'

A pause of shocked surprise, as if their euphoric intro had smashed into a wall. The two psychotherapists from Old Joanna's, Silverman/Klein, had spotted Hayden.

'Oh.' Flat.

'Hi.' Also flat.

Gush turned to glacial. They remained standing and turned back to Marina.

'Sorry. You're with a client. Nos culpae.'

'We spotted him first, but hey.'

'And boy, have you hit the motherlode there.'

'Three mothers? Pun most certainly intended.'

Marina squeezed Hayden's hand and laughed as if this was the funniest thing she'd ever heard.

'Do they mean who I think they mean? Lucky you.' She turned back to Silverman/Klein. 'It was pretty common in Ireland in those days.'

'For sure?'

'Totally for sure,' said Marina. 'I wrote a paper on it. *One Mother Syndrome*. About the psychological trauma experienced by men who felt left out.'

'Wow!'

'Totally wow,' said Marina. 'Oh, and Hayden is not a client.' She squeezed his hand again. 'At least I hope that's not why he's here.'

Silverman/Klein looked confused. They sat, uninvited, down.

'You mean –'

'Let me take this one, Judith. You mean you're romantically in*volved* with this man?'

They leaned towards Marina and spoke as one.
'Now why do you think that is?'

*

Hayden overshot his stop on the way back and was stomping home to cool off, when he registered, subconsciously, a stocky figure emerging from a side street. He stomped on. Bloody nut doctors! The 'session' had segued neatly from his mental health – fascination with – to psychotherapy small talk. Marina had squeezed his hand every few minutes, an it-won't-always-be-like-this squeeze, but three psychotherapists in a huddle for two hours fifty minutes? Shop talk. Fritz Perelman's *Families And How To Avoid Them*? By the time he headed off with a throbbing cranium, Hayden felt as if he'd written the bloody thing.

His footsteps echoed on the pavement as he approached the home stretch. Hold on. Echoed? His footsteps hadn't echoed before. He stomped a bit faster. The echoes sped up. He was starting to panic now. The stocky figure. Pointer? Could it possibly be Detective Chief Inspector Ronnie Pointer, following him, tracking his every move? Typical devious cop. They lull you into a false sense of security, then *wham!* What if he'd got hold of Rich's mobile? Unimpeachable barge pilot to local police to Pointer. A bit far-fetched, but the way Hayden was feeling, far-fetched worked. So, Pointer has the mobile, traces the call from Hayden, discovers Hayden is a comedian and Rich's ex-client, decides to reactivate the case, targets Hayden as the prime suspect –

Hayden's mobile pinged but he didn't hear it. He quickened his steps. The steps behind him quickened too. He ignored the turn for Leverton Street and walked straight on. Shake Pointer off, that was the plan. He quickened his steps. Again. Ditto the steps behind. Hayden was pretty well at Olympic walking race level. Any quicker and he'd be running and that, he felt, was an admission of guilt. He resigned himself to the inevitable and slowed his pace to a stroll. Best get it over with. He could hear the steps behind him, coming closer now. He heard the heavy breathing. He waited for the hand on the shoulder. The *You are well and truly nicked, my son.* But none came. Only the footsteps, relaxing now as they approached their compliant prey.

Hayden braced himself and turned to face his pursuer.

'I invented comedy, me.'

Hayden breathed a heartfelt sigh of relief. 'Of course you did, Baldy,' he said. 'Of course you fucking did.'

# 14

Hayden arrived back at Wolfe's a much-relieved man. It certainly made him think, though, as he grabbed his laptop and sat on the sofa. His heart had been put through it on the short trip out. It had set out to post a letter in romantic mode. On the return journey it was closer to cardiac arrest. Was this fear of being a suspect in Rich's death always going to be there in the background, lurking down a metaphorical side street, ready to pounce?

He opened the laptop and went online. Nothing on the news about any murder enquiry yet, but – bloody hell! The internet was awash with Wolfe. *Invisible Woman*. Was he, wasn't he? The story had gone viral. Wolfe Swift had been spotted in Tucson Arizona, Paris, Cahirciveen. Anywhere, it seemed, but his home address. Nobody seemed to know he had a house in London. That's how private The Greatest Actor Of This Or Any Other Age was.

Hayden located the film trailer. Might find a clue in there. Hint of male voice from the lead? Trace of Dublin accent? He settled back and clicked play. Two hundred years in ninety seconds, but it devoted nearly half of those to *Invisible Woman*'s rendition of *Don't You Drag Your Sorry Ass Back Here*, a 1920's nightclub scene where our invisible protagonist is barred from the venue but sings outside anyway. The band, all white men, played inside, volume pitched to back her through the walls. Wonderful, heartbreaking, invisible singer blues. Stunning performance. But Wolfe Swift? Come *on*.

A follow-up question seemed to be exercising the fans. The Oscar ceremony was less than two weeks away, so would he, wouldn't he?

1 Win.

2 Turn up.

The way the story was developing online, however, it seemed Wolfe Swift had disappeared. It was almost funny when you thought about it. Screenwriting guru Melanie 'Bud' Schultz concocts outlandish scenario for maximum publicity. Actor disappears. New book flies off shelf. But Wolfe Swift as a black, female, American icon? The idea was beyond laughable. *The International Enquirer* didn't seem to think so, however. It carried a shot of Wolfe relaxing in a Tuscaloosa motel in character. Empty room. Rocking chair. Bible. That was their proof.

Well maybe, but also, and this is where I'd put *my* money, maybe not.

Having said that, Wolfe didn't appear to be at home either. Why not? Had he, perhaps, got wind of the online furore? Was he on the run from the paparazzi? The red-top hacks? The mob? A bit disconcerting for Hayden and very bad news if he was. Wolfe was supposed to be concentrating on his next film, not one he'd finished some time back – if, that is, he was in it in the first place. Which, web-induced hysteria notwithstanding, was highly unlikely. Maybe he'd gone off somewhere quiet to learn his lines. Or, although Hayden wasn't to know this, he could still be stuck to a seat at Browse & Quaff, crumbling sugar cubes.

Nothing to be done wherever he was, so Hayden rattled around the house on his own for the next few days, trying to kickstart his next project. He also dropped in to Julius Okeke's office to sort out his new contract. Nothing about triple locks or Largs, so he signed with a flourish in the young, attractive, gender-fluid contracts department and used the word 'actually' twice. He was heading out the door when his mobile pinged.

Incoming text:

*How's the fillum?*

Another text from Bram, his childhood friend in Dublin, but he had no time for Bram now. He'd seen a second text.

*Sorry about that. Those women are seriously disturbed. But you? More please. M xxx*

Triple x? Brilliant! But hold on. The text had been sent shortly after he'd left Marina. When he'd headed off from the Keynote Conference Hotel and she'd crawled, shell-shocked, up to her room to escape the Silverman/Klein effect. In the drama of the moment he'd totally missed her message, and continued to miss it for three whole days. Bloody hell! She'd think he didn't care! So, what to do? Declare his undying love right here on the pavement?

*yes yes yes oh yes triple x?*

On the other hand –

The text from Bram had given him a better idea.

# 15

Dublin in October? Magic. He'd stay at Eddie's house in Clontarf. An excellent bolt-hole for when his Hollywood career got too hot – but right now it was a handy place to go back to. It meant he didn't have to stay with his beloved aunts. Or Bram. It was also across the road from Marina's. Perfect.

I won't dwell on the trip itself. Hayden couldn't find Eddie's house keys before he headed off. Not to worry, though. The three aunts would have a spare set. He also found the contents of his jacket on the bedside table. He was sure he hadn't put them there. To add to his frustration, he couldn't find his jacket. He was sure he'd put it on the back of a chair. Apparently not in all three cases, but for a man this was pretty predictable, so no problem to Hayden. He wore his spare jacket. He also packed a short stay overnight bag. Odd. He seemed to be three pairs of underpants short of the full set. He had six pairs in all, for those interested in matters sartorial. Three gone, one on, two left. Oh well, should be fine. He packed them. Same with socks, but the absence of underwear, for some reason, is more disturbing.[13]

On the plus side, the journey itself was uneventful, for Hayden at least. Tube to Heathrow. Plane. Smooth trip all the way. I couldn't help noticing DCI Pointer stuffing a golf bag into the overhead locker a few rows in front, but Hayden didn't see a thing. He was too busy attempting to feed the beast. His travel notebook, to clarify, was blank.

---

[13] Ref. Professor Emeritus Larry Stern's exquisitely written monograph, *Schrodinger's Underpants*.

Difficult second script blank.

*

At Dublin airport Hayden strolled through customs. No baggage in the hold, so he was first out. As he walked from the bag collection area to the main terminal, he instinctively searched the waiting faces for his lift. Slap on the head time: he hadn't told anyone he was coming. He wound his way through the crowd and headed to the main exit. Bus or taxi? He'd plumped for the expensive option – he'd have to get used to it, possibly with dark glasses – when he almost bumped into Bram.

Bram?!

'What are *you* doing here?' That was Hayden, but it might as well have been Bram.

Bram looked confused, but then, he always looked confused. 'I just saw you off,' he said. 'Didn't I?'

Typical Bram. Early onset something? Difficult to tell. He was probably here to drop off his new love Trace for a nostalgic trip back to Alcoholics Anonymous. He'd leave it, Hayden decided. That was the best way to deal with Bram. Change the subject. So Hayden changed it. 'Any chance of a lift?' he said.

There was every chance of a lift. Bram was heading to Clontarf anyway. He'd drop him right at Eddie's door. 'Again,' said Bram. Hayden didn't follow, but with Bram you didn't need to. Bram, you accepted, was Bram. Again? Have it your way, Bram. Again. They headed towards the car.

Bram was uncharacteristically quiet the whole drive. He kept glancing over at Hayden. Surreptitiously. It reminded Hayden of silent film star Finlay Jameson's posthumous masterpiece, *Silence*, where the same lugubrious twelve-second face shot plays over and over again for 97 minutes, anticipating the birth of the internet gif by the best part of a century.

Unlike Finlay, however, Bram eventually spoke. As he swung in at Eddie's Kincora Road address and parked by the kerb, he glanced over at Hayden.

Surreptitiously.
Again.
'But seriously. I dropped you off at the airport,' he said. 'Didn't I?'

*

Across the road and next door to Marina's, the three aunts were out in their front garden sweeping up dead leaves. They peered at Hayden through the gate. He spotted them and sauntered over.

'Howaya, Hayding.'

'Lo, the weary traveller returns.'

'But from whence?'

'Besides, Hayding, we tought you were here already. We only seen you off about 12 seconds ago.'

'That's the lovely ting about dementia, Hayding. You're always wit us, even when you're not.'

'He *was* here already,' said Bram. 'I dropped him up to the airport.'

But Hayden wasn't listening. He was studying the three aunts as he'd never studied them before. He could almost swear they were the Merrie Spinsters. That's how good the Merries were. 'About Eddie,' he said.

'Terrible news, Hayding.'

'Yes, yes. I know he passed away –' Hayden didn't have time for this.

'In tragic circumstances, Hayding.'

'Done away wit by his only begotting son.'

'So I believe, ladies. So I believe. But I seem to have mislaid his keys.'

'You're worse than us, Hayding.'

'Have you looked in your man bag?'

Bram gave Hayden an odd look and cut across the giggles. 'Mislaid the keys? You gave a set to your man!' he said.

'Your man?' said Hayden. 'Which particular 'your man' are we talking about?'

'The guy with the lorry. The one coming out of Eddie's.'

Hayden glanced across the road. Sure enough, a man had come out the gate and was striding along the path towards them. 'Keys, boss,' he said, thrusting them at Hayden. 'Right. That's us off. Anything else needs shifting, let me know.'

Hayden looked at the keys in his hand. He looked at the man climbing into the lorry and driving off. He'd never met him before in his life. Anything else? Surely 'anything' comes before 'anything else', so what exactly was 'anything'? He was beginning to question his own sanity. On the plus side, he had the keys. He jangled them in front of the three aunts and Bram. 'Sorted,' he said. 'Oh, and thanks for the lift, Bram.'

'Correction,' said Bram. 'Lifts plural.' He chuckled playfully. 'Don't want to miss your plane,' he said. 'Hop in. I'll drop you up to the airport.'

\*

Readers of *Sloot* will be acquainted with Clontarf. For those who haven't read it, Clontarf is Dublin's leafiest suburb. Wonderful spot. I grew up on Kincora Road. So did Hayden. But read *Sloot*. It's all in there. *Hewbris* will wait. Besides, the three aunts were in chatty mode after Bram left, which is almost a book in itself. Length-wise, that is.[14]

Hayden listened politely while they waxed lyrical about the dead leaves reminding them of 'the melancholy impermulence of tings' and 'the immulence of our own det'. 'Wedder we be saint or sinner', 'rich man or poor man', 'or, Hayding', – pause for a fit of giggles here – 'their long-suffering wives'. He left them to their 'morbid prognosticayshings', long after the lorry driver had pulled away. Enormous lorry, by the way. It shouldn't

---

[14] *The Annotated Hewbris* pp. 906-1152.

have been anywhere near a quiet suburban street, but at least it wasn't parked on the grass verge.

Hayden crossed the road and walked up the gravel driveway to Eddie's. He felt a twinge as he put the key in the lock. This was the house he'd grown up in, this was the house where...

Yes, the house where he'd killed Eddie; but any thought of dwelling on feelings of guilt and sorrow fled as soon as he stepped inside. The place had been stripped bare. The furniture, gone. The shelving, gone. No sign of the kettle, or the teapot. He went over to the window and looked out. The shed, gone. Eddie's masterpiece, a magnificent statue which appeared to change human shape depending on the angle of the sun – you may be ahead of me here – gone. Well, at least that explained the lorry.

But these were not what he'd come back for. These were material things, probably put in storage for protective purposes, and they weren't at the forefront of his thoughts. No. Marina was. Marina, and only Marina, was why he'd returned. He had a brief flash forward to wedded bliss: Hayden the successful screenwriter. Marina the stay-at-home mother. Couple of kids. Hayden Junior. Haydena. Toss in the pipe and slippers and you have a pretty conservative, not to say downright reactionary scenario, but you know what they say: you can't edit your deepest desires. Probably best, however, to keep that particular image to himself. Like all practitioners of the comedic arts I've ever met, he didn't like people laughing at him.

But Marina.

Chocolates. He needed a big box of chocolates.

Flowers. He also needed a big bunch of flowers.

And a love card. Valentine's Day was months away, but no harm getting in early.

He tossed his bag onto Eddie's bare floorboards and headed straight back out.

*

The sweetie section in Madden's supermarket. Hayden was weighing up the merits and demerits of a box of Belgian truffles against a king-size Yorkie – the latter was half-price but that was no excuse – when he heard a familiar voice from the drinks aisle.

'Leave the little lady at home, Ronnie. That's what I always say. Golf is a man's game.'

Detective Inspector Lou Brannigan's voice. Lou Brannigan. The very detective who hadn't solved the Uncle Eddie case. And Ronnie? He only knew one Ronnie. Detective Chief Inspector Ronnie Pointer. The chances of it being that particular Ronnie were minimal, but why take the risk? Hayden put the Yorkie bar back in its stand and moved, tentatively, to the end of the aisle to have a closer listen. Bad move. They were out of earshot until, suddenly –

'You are well and truly nicked, my son.' Detectives Inspector Lou Brannigan and Chief Inspector Ronnie Pointer appeared at the far end of the aisle pushing a drink-laden trolley, both resplendent – irony intended – in Argyle sweaters and matching tartan golf trews. But Hayden didn't even notice the outfits. He was rooted to the spot, his fear naked and all-consuming. 'That,' continued Pointer, 'is by way of being my catchphrase. My calling card, if you will.'

'Do you tell me so?' said Brannigan. 'You are well and truly nicked, my son. Well that's a good one all right. That's the business entirely. I'll use that. And speak of the divil,' they'd spotted Hayden, 'if it isn't the man who done away with his very own daddy. Allegedly.'

'Ah, yes,' said Pointer. 'Irish chap. Met him on the mainland.' Then, turning to Hayden, 'Painter and decorator wasn't it, Pat?'

'Oh now,' said Brannigan. 'Is that the way of it? Painter and decorator now, is it? Bit of a fantasist when I knew him anyways.'

Pointer chortled genially. 'Is that a fact, Pat?' he said.

'Lou, Ron,' said Brannigan. 'The name is Lou.'

'Excellent name for a special constable, Pat,' said DCI Pointer. He turned back to Hayden. 'Well, can't stand around chatting all day. The eighteenth hole waits for no man.'

Hayden watched from toiletries, speechless, as Brannigan and Pointer paid up and left. Minutes later he left himself. Paranoid, no chocs.

*

Outside Madden's, Hayden should have turned right and walked briskly towards Marina's, love tokens gift-wrapped by a helpful member of staff. That was the original plan, but the plan had been disrupted by Pointer. Why was he here? There could only be one reason. Couldn't there? Hayden turned left towards the seafront. He was about to get sucked further into the black hole of paranoia. Two hours staring out to sea while he figured out what to do next. To be honest, I was fed up with his internal struggles, and was wondering how best to occupy the angst-ridden interim, when –

'Dere goes Hayding. Off to agonise again.'

'The dark day of the soul.'

'But what about you, Een? We do follow your career wit interest –'

'–as referenced in your estimable novel, *Sloot*, of which more anon.'

'Your stand-up days are now a ting of the past since you opted for the novel form, we deduce.'

'A sad loss to the performing arts, dough. We do quote your act verbatim to brighten doze long winter nights.'

'Cut to *The Joy of Det* at the Edinburgh fridge, Een.'

'Your celebrated foray into the dramaturgical arts.'

'*Very* impressive. Shame it wasn't captured on cellulite.'

'You reminded us of a young Dickie Burting. Bit of a lush, but a sexual atlete of veritably Olympian stamina.'

'Not to mention libidinous appetite. He used to quote *Under Milk Wood* to avoid premature –'

'Dottie! He's a *juvenile*.'

'Florrie. Sorry about that, Een. How old *are* you, by the way?'

'Fifty-two,' I lied.

'You don't look it. But we digress. Following your many tesbian triumphs –'

'– roll of drums –'

'– you wrote your breakout novel, *Sloot*. As previously referenced.'

'Highly wrought as the saying goes. You have a certing facility wit langwidge which suggests you may have found your true calling at last.'

'Which brings us back to *Sloot*'s perfectly realised but somewhat flawed protagonist, Hayding. His constant diddering almost overwhelmed your narrative flow.'

'We refer to drafts one to twelve.'

'Fortunously, however, your device of leaving the plot to look after itself while you pursued your own agenda proved bote structurally serendipitous and pleasingly mirtful.'

I braced myself for a fit of giggles, but they suddenly switched their attention to a point behind my left knee[15]. I turned to see Hayden's retreating back, as he crossed the road onto the seafront and disappeared along the promenade. No giggles from the three aunts, but rather an empathetic sigh.

'Poor old Hayding. If only he knew what was coming.'

They froze at this, as if they'd given voice to the last thing they wanted to say.

'How do you mean?' I asked.

'Oh nutting, Een.'

'*Rien de rien* as Edit Piaf used to say, many's the time and oft, during our lengty Parisian sojourn.'

I coughed politely to ease them back to the present. No effect.

---

[15] A humorous reference to their tininess.

'Did we ever tell you about our little *ménage à quatre* during the nineteen forty tree blackout –'

'*Cinq*, Flottie. Don't forget Maurice Chevalier of more than blessèd memory.'

'Ah yes, ah remember *E 12*, Een. His musical love letter to Londing's Wanstead Flats.'

'I think you'll find Flottie is Dorrie,' I interjected.

Not that I had a clue who was who, but I had to staunch the flow. It worked.

'Janey, is that the time? We have to get back.'

'We've just remembered, Een. We left our whale-bone corsets on the boil.'

Sheepish at this blatant lie[16] they began to retrace their steps, guilt written all over their tiny, aunt-shaped backs.

\*

*If only he knew what was coming.* Difficult to know what to make of that as the three aunts shuffled off homewards. No time to think about that now, however. I had work to do, and it turns out I was right about Hayden. He sat on the seafront wall. Pining for Marina. Festering over Pointer. Glowering at the outgoing tide.

Happily, however, the fates conspired to move things dramatically on. Hayden glanced at his watch. Might be time to self-flagellate over a flat white in the Nautical Buoy. He turned away from the water and glowered at the promenade instead. A few kids kicked a ball around. Strollers, relaxed and meditative, headed nowhere in particular and, crossing the road at the Vernon Avenue traffic lights – Hayden recognised her immediately – Marina. She spotted him, smiled and waved. Her pace quickened. Hayden brightened. She was pleased to see him. He stood as she approached. She quickened her pace

---

[16] Monday for corset boiling. Always Monday.

and put her arms around him, almost proprietorially, as if this was the most natural thing in the world.

'I thought you were going back to London,' she said, 'but I'm very glad you didn't.' Hayden was puzzled. He had gone back to London. Weeks ago. There was something about this apparent intimacy, something not quite right. But he didn't know what it was. Then, suddenly, he did. Wolfe Swift *is* Hayden McGlynn. Jesus! The jacket. The underpants. The socks. Bram's 'Again.'

Marina moved closer. 'Last night,' she smiled. 'Last night was really beautiful.' Then her smile was coloured by a slightly quizzical frown. 'But that phone call. About killing your agent.' She leaned over and kissed his stunned left cheek. 'You were joking. Right?'

# 16

The three aunts' parting words resounded in Hayden's ears as he headed back to the airport the following day for the first available flight. *Will you look at him, the craytur. You'd tink he'd been hit be a bombsite.* He had. He had. Okay, so Wolfe Swift was playing Hayden McGlynn, but what the libidinous bastard had done was positively *despicable*. To add to Hayden's misery, Bram gave him a lift to the airport. Bram wasn't the problem, his other passenger was. Bram's new love, Trace, sat in the back, her very presence adding to Hayden's woes. He grunted at Trace as he got in and left it at that.

As Bram reached the end of Kincora Road and turned right towards Killester, a large makeshift sign flapped in the breeze across the gatehouse of Clontarf Castle. *International Police Conference & Golfing Weekend.* Golf. Pointer had been over for... *golf*. Nothing to do with Hayden after all. But his relief at this news was as nothing compared to – he couldn't finish the sentence, even mentally. Wolfe Swift. The Greatest Actor Of This Or Any Other Age has to *live* the fucking part! Had he never heard of acting? Worse, he had to live it with Marina! The only woman Hayden had ever truly – he couldn't finish that sentence either. I mean, I mean, what if he was playing Herod? Hoh? Didn't mean he had to charge round Egypt slaughtering the new-fucking-*born*!

Hayden kept all this to himself as they reached the top of Castle Avenue. Professor Emeritus Larry Stern on his bike flew past on the inside, a long woollen scarf in the colours of his imaginary university fluttering behind him in the breeze.

I'd wisely packed a copy of *The Quintessential Stern* for the journey back and would, no doubt, relax with a few pages on the plane while Hayden festered and wept. For now, though, he sat scowling through the front window, clenching and unclenching his apoplectic fists.

As Bram turned left onto Howth Road, a hand appeared over the back of the seat and squeezed Hayden's shoulder. Solicitously. 'You're doing great, Hayden,' said Trace. This was the icing on the misery cake, and Hayden knew what was coming next. 'God says thanks.' Another solicitous squeeze. 'He's been keeping an eye on things and He knows you're fighting the good fight, keeping off the sauce.'

'There's no God, lady. We're tiny, meaningless dots in a dark, meaningless universe, and Wolfe Swift is a cunt.' Hayden didn't say that. What was the point? Besides, Bram had taken up the conversational slack.

'She's right, Haydo. Fight the good fight. You know? I mean, speaking man to man, some people are better off the jungle juice. You know?' This all sounded a bit forced, as if he'd been prepped by Trace. He patted Hayden's knee. 'Anyway, jury's out on the God bit, but Trace is right. You're doing good.' He glanced through the rear-view mirror. 'That right, sweetheart?'

'No, Bram,' said Trace. 'The jury delivered its verdict *years* ago. Plus he's not doing good.' She leaned forward and squeezed Hayden's shoulder again. 'He's doing *great*.'

Hayden ground his teeth. 'That's great, Trace,' he said. 'We're all doing great.'

'Great,' said Trace.

Bram shifted gears and concentrated on driving. Hayden sat rigid and silent. A doom-laden silence broken only, as the car pulled up at Dublin Airport, by a tiny voice from the back.

'God says well done.'

\*

The plane banked and rose in the clear blue sky. Below, the stunning coastline from Howth to the Wicklow mountains and beyond. It wheeled over Dollymount and the Bull Wall, that raised pathway with bathing shelters leading out to sea. At its end a towering statue of the Blessed Virgin Mary. Bit of an anachronism in modern Ireland? Time, perhaps, to replace it with Eddie's masterpiece, that stunningly innovative sculpture celebrating iconic Irishwomen through the ages with each shift of sunlight and shadow; women who had made a lasting contribution to Irish culture for better or better still? Eddie had offered it to the nation, but it had been rejected by the powers-that-be and had instead languished in his back garden for decades.

I mused on this in a distracted sort of way. I opened *The Quintessential Stern* at a random page, and was soon lost in its limpid prose and stunningly provocative theses. At one point the learned professor refers to tragedy as comedy's sulky sibling. He also admits, and this certainly amused *me*, that he's never laughed himself: 'I was always too busy taking notes.' But it's his proof of the existence of God in the addendum, *Level Six*, that had me reeling. This is too serious a subject to relegate to a footnote, so let me deal with it head on: Stern posits five levels of comedy. Five. Yet here, in *Level Six*, he adds a theoretical level espousing the existence, nay, the *provable* existence, of a supreme being. As a non-believer I was, to say the least, profoundly shocked. But I'm a passionate proponent of free speech and am open, I sincerely hope, to new ideas and having my mind changed by rigorous and forthright debate. Herewith is Stern's theory in essence or, given the title of his book, quintessence:

Level One comedy, huge audience. Unsophisticated, coarse, Lowest Common Denominator stuff. Example: Little Jimmy launched his bestselling *Christmas Cracker Gang Rape Joke Book* to an ecstatic audience of Misogynists' Rights bigwigs and their guilt-by-association lady wives in Clacton. By their followers shall ye know them. With Levels Two, Three, and

Four, we witness an increase in the degrees of sophistication and matching decrease in audience numbers. So far, so Stern. In simple terms, the more sophisticated the joke, the smaller the fan base. I'm delighted to report that my own comedy audience has always been pleasingly minute. Little wonder, then, that several of my more recherché efforts are referenced at Level Five.

Level Six introduces a whole new level of incomprehensibility. The ultimate joke. A joke so brilliant, so perfect, so stunningly impenetrable, that no mortal being could possibly understand it. Inference? No mortal being could possibly have written it. Ipso facto? © God. QED. I'll give him this: Stern is clever. Was it not Pascal[17] who suggested that the ultimate proof of the existence of God is that you can't *dis*prove it? As with Pascal, so with Stern. I took issue with his thesis, yet found it impossible to refute.

But let's leave it there for the moment and get back to Hayden. Lulled by a mixture of extreme angst and the plane's gentle throb, he'd fallen sound asleep, a nightmare lying in wait: Wolfe Swift. In bed. With Marina. The nightmare dwells on the climax of their lovemaking. On a loop. In erotic detail, sadly, not to mention glorious technicolour and equally glorious sensurroundsound. Several loops in Hayden managed to jerk himself awake, but soon afterwards, lulled again as above, he slept on. Cue *The Nightmare: Part Two*. Wolfe arrives back in London following his illicit love tryst and is recognised by the baying mob, furious that he's breached a code of film ethics by taking the lead in *Invisible Woman*. White Irishman plays iconic African-American woman? What was he *thinking*? He's dragged from the plane to a magnolia tree which has mysteriously sprouted through the arrivals lounge, placed on a horse beneath the strongest bough, and strung up. Close-up on his face.

He's not Wolfe Swift.

---

[17] Not mother-killer Pascal O'Dea from *Sloot*. Different Pascal. Accent on the second syllable.

He's Hayden.

They've got the wrong man.

Hayden jerked awake, as the horse was kicked away and the plane was about to land. The wheels hit the tarmac with a jolt, the plane taxied along the runway, rain streaming across the windows. People stirring all around. Seatbelts unfastening. Muzak. Hayden steadied himself as he grabbed his overnight bag and joined the queue for the exit. At least, he reflected, things couldn't get any worse.

# 17

First rule of comedy? Things can always get worse. Relax, though. Happy ending guaranteed. Having said that, happiness is relative: different things to different people. This particular happy ending works for me, though. Last page if you can't wait, but what's the point? You won't know why it's happy.

# 18

Hayden festered all the way home on the tube. That's two changes, 26 stops. By the second change he was ready to kill someone, and he knew who that someone was. As he left the tube and strode home he gripped his overnight bag with malice aforethought. Incandescence washed over him in waves. His career hung in the balance. So, what to do? Kill Wolfe? In his present state of mind it seemed like the logical thing to do. Then he had a better idea. He'd phone Julius Okeke. Suggest a change of cast. Bit of a long shot, but a long shot was still a shot. Besides, it was Hayden's script. Any decent actor of a certain age with a good technique and a passable Dublin accent could play Hayden. But no-one else could write him. He punched the number in.

'You are a lucky man, Hayden McGlynn. Today I have two important calls. The first call is completed, the second yet to come. You have precisely thirty-seven seconds.'

Hayden got straight to the point. 'I can't work with Wolfe Swift.' His voice faltered slightly. A tragic exhalation. Not exactly a sob, but close. 'He – he did a very bad thing.' Bit weak on the verbals, but full of authentic feeling.

Julius Okeke sighed on the other end of the line. The empathy sigh. 'Ah, my esteemed and dearest friend. Permit me to formulate my response with a little story. When I was growing up in Malawi my father, too, did a very bad thing. Do you know what that thing was?' Rhetorical question. 'When I was six years old, he took me on a journey. A long, long journey. Me and my beloved father. Oh, I was a happy, happy boy. We bonded, me and my father, my father and me, we bonded over this journey, this long, long journey. But then? He did the very bad thing of which I speak. And do you know what that bad thing was? I will tell you, Hayden McGlynn. I will tell you what that bad thing was. He deposited me in the lion enclosure at Serengeti National Park.[18] To this very day I remember his sorrowful face as he waved his heartfelt goodbye. He was sad, Hayden McGlynn. Heartbroken. So why? Why had he done this terrible thing that made him sad? I truly had to know, so when I finally reached home, much scarred from my terrible experiences, I asked my father, "Why, Father? Why did you do this terrible thing that made you sad?" And do you know what he answered, Hayden McGlynn? I will tell you. "Trust me, my youngest and most precious son," replied my father. "I did it to teach you the most important lesson you must learn in this cold and pitiless world. Trust no-one." I have learned that lesson, and you must learn it too, because my father did a very bad thing, but he also did a very good thing. In those twelve years I spent trying to find my childhood home, Hayden McGlynn, I became a man. Call on the other line.'

And Julius Okeke was gone.

Whatever lay ahead, Hayden's fate, and that of his nemesis Wolfe Swift, were inextricably linked.

---

[18] There's no lion enclosure at Serengeti National Park. Julius Okeke is simply living his truth. And not for the first time.

# 19

As Hayden passed Old Joanna's on the home stretch, he was back to thoughts of murder, which puts him pretty definitively in the anti-hero camp. Murder, after all, is not nice, and murderers, by implication, not nice people. He'd already killed his own flesh and blood, remember. But this raises an interesting question. Are we to judge his oeuvre by his actions? Should our understanding of his terrible deed colour our appreciation of the brilliant career he may be about to embark on? I am reminded of an overheard remark at *Adolf Hitler: The Self-Portraits*, in Tate Liverpool. *Holocaust? Bad business I grant you, but look at the way he captures that moustache.* Or how about revered comedian Big Al Konigsberg, who married his biological grandchild at the age of ninety. Bit dodgy to some ways of thinking, but should it detract from the fact that he wrote a superb one-liner in the late sixties? My point? See Hayden as a prospective double-murderer and read on accordingly or, alternatively, see him as a flawed but potentially great artist and ditto.

This book, I like to think, works both ways.

\*

Hayden turned the corner into Leverton Street. A steady stream of workmen, some in paint-spattered overalls, were filing out of Wolfe's front door. Tins of paint. Toolboxes. Stepladders. They finished loading up the van as Hayden passed. One of them tipped his woolly cap as he clambered into the driver's seat. 'Nice timing, guv. All done and dusted.'

Guv? Hayden? Ah. Bloody Wolfe again. He gave the driver a cursory nod as he drove off, went to the front door and put the key in the lock. But as he was about to turn it, he heard a noise. A scratching noise. It patently wasn't Wolfe so who, or what, was it? The noise got louder and more insistent. Followed by a low, insistent whine.

He opened the letter box for a quick peek and Eddie's beloved dog Rusty, yes, Rusty the thoroughbred mongrel, left to Hayden after Eddie's death, leapt up to greet him. Ye Gods! I hope there are no dog lovers reading this. Hayden, driven by his blind ambition, had left Rusty with the three aunts in Clontarf when he moved back to London, and not a thought given to the poor mutt since. So what was he doing in London now? This was getting beyond disturbing. As Hayden opened the door, Rusty gave him the full welcome-home works and bounded happily into the living room, barking with joy.

If Rusty was a shock to Hayden's system, worse was waiting. The open-plan living room, once bright, airy and modern, was now Eddie's Dublin residence to the life. Mushroom-coloured paint; grey, lifeless curtains; and cluttered with Eddie's furniture. Old, worn, decrepit. It even seemed to have come supplied with a generous layer of dust. So *that* was it; the contents of Eddie's bungalow had been moved en masse to Wolfe Swift's North London address. The artworks. The faded sofa. The teapot.

Hayden sniffed. They'd even got the musty, old-man smell exactly right.

To add to his list of woes, Hayden had just got a text.

*You? Me? Us?*

There was more, but he stopped reading there. His eyes had misted over. He knew immediately who it was from. Marina. For Hayden, in his present frazzled state, this was bordering on psychological torture. Solution? He'd pop into Old Joanna's for a therapeutic blast of Steve: barman, philosopher, friend. Sunday afternoon. It should be pretty quiet in there. Might help to take his mind off things.

Not to mention other things.

\*

Baldy Mayle sat in the corner staring into his glorious past. Apart from that, Steve was alone. He nodded a greeting as Hayden came in. 'How's tricks?' he said.

'Not the best,' said Hayden. 'You know. Things. Other things.'

'Always the way,' said Steve. 'Bit like life.'

'It *is* life, Steve,' said Hayden.

Steve stroked his chin. 'True,' he said. 'True. Speaking of which, shouldn't you be up on the Heath?'

He nodded vaguely in the direction of the poster on the far wall.

# Comedians For World Peace

Several Big Names
Hayden McGlynn
Very Special Guest – Little Jimmy Lawrie
Compère – Bo Bell
Sun. Sept. 27. 2pm
Hampstead Heath

Free But Bring Your Bank Details

Hayden whacked the side of his head. The 'Shit!' whack. He'd forgotten all about it. He glanced at his wrist. 'Jesus. What time is it?'

'Showtime,' said Steve. 'Hail a cab.'

Baldy smiled enigmatically and hugged his empty glass. 'I invented comedy, me,' he said.

Hayden's thoughts were elsewhere as the outside door swung shut. Steve switched his attention back to the counter, which didn't need wiping, but he wiped it anyway. It stopped him from thinking about life. 'Course you did, Baldy,' he said absently. 'Course you did.'

*

'Taxi!'

A black cab did an illegal U-turn and screeched to a halt. Hayden hopped in. The cab pulled out. The driver was off. Strong Crumlin accent.[19]

'Course it's noh a black cab *as such*.' He squinted through the rear-view mirror. 'I seen you somewhere before, righ'? Hold on a sec. Hellfire Club. Up the Dublin mountains, yeh? Buryin the bruddah. Oh, and you and the poncy fuck in Clon-fucken-torf. Have you placed now.' So had Hayden. The 'poncy fuck' was Quilty, *aka* Wolfe Swift in his previous role. The cab driver was Grego Pope of notorious Dublin criminals the Pope clan. They raced along Kentish Town Road. 'Had to leave the country meself. Botch job in Harold's Cross. The wife is fucken furious a-course. Nice little numbah this, though. Always testin' The Knowledge. Go on, ask me anythin'. Somewhere to somewhere fucken else.'

Hayden was terrified. He'd hoped never to see the Pope brothers again. He was also in a hurry. 'Old Joanna's in Kentish Town to Hampstead Heath.'

Grego Pope snorted with delight. 'Haven't a fucken clue.'

'Okay,' said Hayden. 'It's back the other way. Straight up the Highgate Road. I'll say when.'

'Grab a fucken lifebelh,' roared Grego, shifting up a gear. 'I'm on ih.'

The cab squealed round and raced back the way it had come. Past Old Joanna's, on towards Highgate, quick lurch to the left. Terrifying minutes later, Hayden stuck his head up to the glass panel. 'You can drop me here,' he shouted politely. 'Thanks.' The cab screeched to a halt. Hayden rooted in his pocket.

---

[19] Dublin. Only more so.

'So, whah's the story?' said Grego, turning to look at Hayden. 'Huge crowd up the hill there. Bih early for funerals, like.'

'Charity gig,' said Hayden. He opened the door to clamber out. 'I'm doing some stand-up.'

'I'll tell you one thing,' said Grego. 'You wouldn' geh *me* up there.'

'Me neither,' muttered Hayden and, all thoughts of settling up forgotten in the tension of the moment, set off up the hill.

Grego Pope opened the window and leaned out. 'I'll keep the meher runnin',' he yelled. 'Break a fucken leg.'

\*

As Hayden made his way up Parliament Hill he could see the crowd in the distance, backlit by beautiful late September sunlight. Blue sky hinting at melancholy, sun like liquid gold.

Big crowd. Probably best served by volume. Not best served, you'd be forgiven for thinking, by Stern Level Five. Outdoor concert and cerebral don't mix. Level One with drum and bass backing? Perfect. But then he remembered. He was a screenwriter now and besides, his last gig at Old Joanna's had been a bit of a stormer. So why not get out there and do the business? He could use a bit of positive in his life. He clenched his fists and started to psych himself up.

He was close to the back of the crowd, and had started to squeeze his way through when Bo took the mic. He brushed past a woman with a bucket.

'Sorry,' he said, 'I'm due onstage.'

'Course you are, love,' said the woman. 'Skinflint.'

The rest of her words, none of them charitable, were drowned out by the gusty breeze and Bo. 'Sad news,' she said. 'Little Jimmy Lawrie couldn't make it today, bless him.'

Straight in with her running gag. The audience responded with one voice. 'Why's that, Bo?'

'Well, I can't go into detail as we have minors present. Usual reason, though. Coach-load of squaddies off to defend the realm in some poor sodding country that's never heard of us. They spot Little Jimmy. Big fans. Act out one of his less family-friendly jokes in a deserted hangar at Heathrow. After that, comedy is the last thing on Lil J's mind.' A roar of mock-sympathy from the crowd as Hayden forced his way through. 'And speaking of comedy, we have a pretty impressive line-up for you this afternoon! But before I introduce our first act, a cautionary tale. Interesting little illustration of the male libido. I walked here, right? Passed under some scaffolding near Kentish Town tube. Sunday afternoon, but there's no escape. Few double-timers working away at roof level. "Cleavage alert below, lads." Cleavage? I was wearing a duffel coat at the time. Toggled up, mark you, to the chin. It gets worse. "I'd give you one, darlin'." What am I supposed to say? Thanks? You flatter me, kind sir? Now fortunately, I always carry a hacksaw in my clutch-bag. Whipped it out. Set to work. Seconds before the whole edifice came crashing down, the culprit slid to safety screaming for his mammy. Irish guy. Not your typical scaffolder I'd have to say. But why am I telling you all this? Because here he is! Please welcome to the stage, comedian, screenwriter and roofer extraordinaire – Hayden McGlynn!'

WHAT?!!!

Why hadn't she got someone else to open? Hayden's elbowing became more frantic as he tried to force his way through the crowd to the stage.

'Scuse me, scuse me. I'm Hayden McGlynn. Scuse me.'

A man in a parka pointed at the side of the stage with his bucket-free hand. 'I think you'll find *that's* Hayden McGlynn,' he said.

He shook the bucket under Hayden's nose, but Hayden was temporarily distracted. Slouching towards the microphone, staring out into the sea of expectant faces, was, well, him.

\*

Onstage Hayden, *aka* Wolfe Swift, was good-looking in a louche sort of way. Bit like me. The words dry, laconic, cerebral might best describe his comic schtick. He launched into an alcohol-related riff about a lost weekend in Scrabster with the bass player from The Clits. An extended shaggy-dog story about picking up all the bacchanalian details from the subsequent court case. Result? Mild titters. He'd told it once too often. He knew this and they, the audience, fed off his lethargy. A smattering of confused laughter, as if they didn't quite know why they were laughing.

He abandoned the sorry tale with a heavily edited ending and was about to segue into a routine about discovering he wasn't Jewish – the only penis reference in his entire oeuvre – when Hayden, still trying to squeeze his way through the crowd, couldn't take it any more. 'I've just had a great idea,' he shouted. 'Why don't you say something funny?'

Hayden froze. Was this not a direct reprise of the scene at the start of *Sloot*? The Scrabster riff. The confused laughter. The heckle. 'Why don't you say something funny?' Exactly what a member of the audience had shouted at Hayden, and now he was shouting it at himself. He couldn't deal with the mental fallout – what did it say about his sanity? He turned and forced his way back through the crowd the way he'd come, with bucket man's words following him out.

'Tight-fisted cunt.'

'And world peace to you too, brother.'

Good riposte, but Hayden didn't say it. His thoughts, as he quit the scene, were dark, nightmarish and elsewhere.

# 20

Hayden stomped down Parliament Hill thinking foul thoughts. He could kill Wolfe Swift. He *would* kill Wolfe Swift. Wolfe Swift was the root of all his woes. If not for Wolfe he could be living rent-free at Eddie's writing his follow up novel and seeing Marina. Not as his psychotherapist, because if Wolfe Swift hadn't come on the scene he wouldn't need one. Pipe. Slippers. Marina. Such a beautiful, peaceful reverie, and eminently achievable on a successful novelist's earnings; but it all seemed so long ago.

Let's consider Hayden for a moment, because there's something I want to clear up. Hayden is, technically, a murderer – even if the murder was committed in such a drunken stupor that Hayden himself can't remember it. Worse, perhaps, is the fact that the man he murdered was his own father, although to be fair Hayden thought Eddie was his uncle at the time. But still. Uncles are people too.

Having said that, Hayden is a rare talent although deeply – and I say this in all humility – influenced by me. No harm in that. We're all influenced by others. I was influenced by – well, I can't think of anyone offhand, but you take my point.

He continued on his way down the hill, fuming. Past Grego Pope snoozing in the driver's seat of his cab, meter still running. Down Highgate Road. Past Old Joanna's, where Detective Chief Inspector Ronnie Pointer was standing outside, busily examining the festival poster and taking notes.

As he stomped past the venue DCI Pointer chuckled in his direction. 'Cracking line-ups, Pat.'

Great. That was all he needed. Pointer studying comedians? He was obviously back on the case. As if Wolfe Swift appropriating Hayden's life wasn't bad enough, Hayden himself could be done for murdering his ex-agent, a murder he hadn't committed. Was that Rich's final joke? He had Hayden tied up in life, and now, in death, he was planning his next twenty years. Why else would DCI Pointer be taking notes about a poster with Hayden's name on it?

Hayden ignored Pointer's remark and stormed manically on. Pedestrians gave him a wide berth. He oozed menace. He was about to barge into a genial drunk, fists deep in his jacket pockets, when two disembodied voices forced their way through to his frontal lobes.

'Not *want*, Hayden.'

'*Need*.'

Silverman/Klein. Standing at the foot of their stairs. Hayden almost screeched to a halt. Here he was, racing along, intent on murdering The Greatest Actor Of This Or Any Other Age. Maybe he *did* need help.

\*

Silverman Klein's office was their first floor Kentish Town flat, directly above the late-night grocer. Hayden followed the two psychiatrists up the stairs. Silverman. Klein. Same outfits. Glasses. Hair. They dispensed with preliminaries in the living-room-stroke-office and sat upright on straight-backed chairs, examining their prey. Hayden sat upright on a chaise longue. They tried getting him to drape, twice, but he always ended back upright, like psychotherapeutic Subbuteo.

Silverman. Klein. Both watching Hayden eagerly as he unburdened himself in this impromptu therapy session. Guilt-induced remorse over killing his father. 'Now why do you think you did that?' Innocence-induced paranoia over not killing his agent. 'Now why do you think you feel that?'

It all poured out unbidden. The traumatic episode with Marina. Seeing himself onstage. His nemesis: Wolfe Swift. The man who had it all. Looks. Talent. Work ethic. An uncanny ability to inhabit whatever character he was playing. And Marina.

This hurt. This hurt so very, very bad.

He'd begun to explore his feelings on the Wolfe/Hayden/Marina love triangle fiasco when Silverman, or possibly Klein, cut across his pain-riven flow.

'So, what are you saying? You cuckolded *yourself*?'

They both started scribbling furiously, their brazen self-interest yanking Hayden back from the world of his deepest feelings to the neon-bright office. He noticed, on the otherwise bare wall, a framed book cover mock-up.

*Multiple Mother Syndrome*

*Silverman Klein*

*'Follow that, Sigmund!'* – New York Times Review of Books

Klein – could have been Silverman – caught his gaze and put her pen down.

'Oh, that. We're working on it. Up to now we've established the following. Judith?'

'Okay. Typically, there are three types of mother. The mother we love, the mother we hate, the mother we have. Other Judith?'

'Okay two, your case. Did you have three physically separate mothers or were all three manifestations contained in the one corporeal frame?'

Hayden put his emotions on hold. These women clearly had no interest in his pain. They were simply using him to further their careers, using his emotions as a case study for their book. Which upset him. No, it annoyed him. A lot. He processed this instead, then gave vent to his rage. But Hayden was a Clontarf boy, and upbringing will out: he vented politely. 'Tell you what,' he said. 'You never know, I might suffer from False Memory Syndrome. Why not ask the mothers themselves?'

'Really?'

'You'd allow us to access the mothers?'

Hayden shrugged. 'Why not?'

'Wow. Breakthrough alert.'

Hayden held his hand out. '*Your* mobile, if that's okay. I might have to leave before you've finished the call. I have a pressing appointment on Tuesday week.'

Judith handed him a phone. Hayden punched the three aunts' number in. They answered before the first ring.

'Hayding. You've invested in a new phone. Tings must be on the sweet up-and-up.'

'Not my phone, ladies. I'd like to pass you over to a couple of psychotherapists for a quick chat.'

'Psychoterapists? Oh, now.'

He put the mobile on speaker and gave it to Silverman. Or possibly Klein. Let's call her Judith. He was pretty furious with both of them and this was an exquisite revenge. In fact, he almost felt sorry for them. Judith adjusted her enormous glasses and was about to speak, which was as far as she got for the rest of the call. The three aunts, as they had been since this paragraph started, were in full flow.

Here's the potted version:

'Of course Hayding says psychoterapist, but possibly unbeknownst to him there are tree distinct and separate disciplines in the treatment of the huming psyche.'

'Psychos terapy, analysis and ology.'

'Not that we know the difference between these highly skilled disciplines ourselves, being mere amatyoors –'

'– but we have had the great honour of intimate relations with Herrs Freud and Jung.'

'Bote of whom, let it be said, were superlative lovers and, in the early stages at least, inseparable, nay *bosom* friends.'

'Sadly, howsomever, they had a falling out.'

'Which was put down, in the generally accepted version, to diverging and ultimately irreconcilable approaches to working metods.'

'Not so. They had a pretty intense daddy/son relationship, and it couldn't bear the added weight of carnal knowledge of the tree aforementioned ladies, namely ours truly.'

The Judiths looked merely shell-shocked at this stage. Give it a while longer, though, and they'd be fit for treatment themselves. This gave Hayden a certain warped satisfaction as he stood up and made for the door. And was it any wonder? He came in wanting to kill Wolfe Swift. He left wanting to kill Wolfe Swift. He hadn't found the help he'd been after.

As if to compound his misery he took his mobile out and read Marina's text in full for the first time.

*You? Me? Us? x?*

That *?* after *x* hit him hard, but he couldn't bear to speak to her, not after what she'd done – not that she knew she'd 'done' *anything*. He pressed delete and walked downstairs as Lindsey the hairdresser stamped past, in what looked like a terrible mental state, to the chaise longue of Silverman/Klein. He made fleeting eye contact with Hayden, and his look was heart-rendingly haunted, and heart-breakingly sad.

# 21

The following weeks passed in a blur. Wolfe Swift was immersed in being Hayden – the Hayden of the *Bad Blood* script, living out Hayden's former stand-up career and the events of Uncle Eddie's murder – and Hayden was filled with foul but unexecuted thoughts of killing Wolfe. He kept to his bedroom, but gone were the luxury bed and duvet, the goose down pillow, the Kandinski print that wasn't a print. No, the bedroom was now an exact replica of his childhood bedroom at Eddie's. Hayden had been catapulted, like a waking nightmare, straight back into his childhood.

The lights were a riot of tiny pinpoints, dotted into the ceiling like multi-coloured stars; the Plough and the Milky Way jumbled together in a crazy, playful pattern. Shelves lined the far wall, stacked with Eddie-made, Hayden-friendly toys. The duvet cover had a young Hayden woven abstractly into the fabric, hands behind his head, looking dreamily up at the night sky. And it all bore down on Hayden. The lights like needles sticking into his eyeballs, the shelves and duvet like accusations from beyond the grave.

The sight outside the bedroom window gave Hayden no relief from his mental torture. A much smaller garden than Eddie's – this was London after all, not Clontarf – but Eddie's neglected masterpiece was a perfect fit. It had been transported, along with the shabby contents of his house, from Eddie's back garden to Wolfe Swift's London address. It was almost surreal. No plinth, so as statues go it was pretty discreet and, like in Clontarf, as Hayden was soon to discover, it seemed to change its appearance to suit the time of day. By the light of the mid-afternoon sun, for example – 3.32pm to be precise – it bore a striking resemblance to Augusta, Lady Gregory, who ran a salon for many years in this very city.

Hayden spent his days and nights pacing, festering, sleeping fitfully. Not an idea in his head that wasn't murderous. But murderous thoughts are one thing, murderous actions another. Cut to day six. The moon was full. It lit up the statue with a metallic glow. At 1.34am it resembled, to Hayden's eyes, all twelve members of the notorious Shankill Butchers. None of them female. Disturbing, certainly, and symptomatic of his inner turmoil, because to anyone else it looked like Bridie Gallagher.

He wasn't sure what he was seeing any more, so at 1.35am, torn between anger and tears, he went downstairs. Wolfe sat on Eddie's sofa, fists clenched, staring at his laptop. Beside the sofa, a crate of Uncle Eddie's *Sweet Ambrosia*. Hayden could almost smell the fumes through the caps on the bottles. Could almost taste the sweet oblivion. What was to stop him prising a bottle out, drinking the contents, and smashing it over Wolfe Swift's insufferable head, spilling his brains on the varnished oak floor? Oh, sweet release! He stood behind Wolfe for some time, trembling with uncontrollable rage. He had to get out of there, fast, or blood would be shed. Rusty gave him a pleading look as he headed to the front door, but this was no time for a dog walk. He slipped out and closed the door behind him. 1.42am.

\*

On the other end of the line, Bram yawned. He'd called Bram because Bram was a good listener. But 1.51am? 'Bit late, plus this is all a bit, you know, heavy. Hold on a sec.' Hayden stomped down Kentish Town Road and waited, his mobile clamped to his ear. 'Still there? Okay. Trace says something about – hold on. Oh, Right. Something about the seven stages of whatsit. Sobriety. You're at number five. Anger. Well done, by the way. Two to go. Plus God says thou shalt not kill. Got that?'

Hayden got that. Thank you Bram. Goodnight. And he supposed God was right, on this one at least. Let's face it: Hayden was never going to kill Wolfe Swift. He wasn't the type for the real, premeditated thing. Too calculated. He'd swatted a fly as a small child and never really got over it. So, murder was out, no matter how riddled with anger he was, but the problem remained. By sleeping with Marina, Wolfe Swift had destroyed his best chance of happiness on the love front. How best to deal with this? The answer came courtesy of London Transport.

It was a dark night. Moody lighting. The odd car. Hayden lost in thought. A night bus passing by. On the side of the bus – a poster for *Invisible Woman*. Brilliant marketing: a lone mic stand with no-one behind it. That was it. Hayden's mind, so recently fixated on murder, took a sudden detour. He felt energised. *Invisible Woman*: identity of actress. Because of *course* there was someone behind the mic stand! Let's say it *was* Wolfe Swift. What if, instead of killing Swift, Hayden grassed him up? White man plays black woman? Here's his address, media vultures. Camp outside. Expose him. Destroy him.

Hayden, as he marched menacingly along, was now enraged by the obscene levels of white appropriation in the film industry. It had never particularly bothered him before, but hell, it bothered him now. He seethed with righteous indignation. It was an abomination that cried to heaven for retribution. First slavery, now this. Well it stopped right here, and it stopped right now. He, Hayden McGlynn, would make a stand on behalf of his brethren and sisthren of colour everywhere. He wielded the metaphorical sword of righteousness as he seethed past a stationary cab.

'How'd it go, head?' Grego Pope. Leaning against the cab in the early-hours darkness as if he knew, with a Pope's unerring instinct for such things, that Hayden would eventually pass by. The Grego Popes of this world know that everyone of interest eventually passes by. All you have to do is leave the meter running and wait. Hayden had forgotten all about Grego, the cab ride and settling up, and yes, he'd left the meter running, as he promised Hayden he would. He didn't even bother looking at it. 'Three six zero, pal. Sterlin'. Leh's say half a grand, hoh? Round ih up, like.'

Five hundred pounds? Christ! Old Joanna's to Hampstead Heath? He'd have walked the cab ride in ten minutes. This was crazy. Except it wasn't. It was Popeland. Euros in Dublin, sterling in London, but they always came out on top.

Hayden didn't have five hundred pounds. He'd maxed out his credit card. His overdraft was only three hundred. Grego grinned at him. This was problematic. He could always do a runner, but if Hayden was going to commit suicide he'd prefer to do it himself. If Grego Pope was to help out it would probably involve his testicles and a mangle, and he really didn't want to involve his testicles for personal reasons, so he said he'd need to go to a cash machine. Grego pointed at the wall behind him. 'There you go, head,' he said. 'Fucken jackpoh.'

Hayden's hands were trembling again as he tried to locate the card slot. He didn't have the money. He knew he didn't have the money, and pretty soon Grego Pope, leading member of the most feared criminal family in Dublin, would know that too. He felt an excruciating pain in the aforementioned. Psychosomatic at this stage, but Hayden was desperate not to draw attention to them. He covered the screen to protect his pin number as Grego Pope lounged happily against the bonnet of the cab. Grego didn't need the pin number. That was Hayden's job.

Hayden pressed the button for five hundred cash. He waited. The card popped out. The money followed. He couldn't believe it. He pushed the card back in. Pressed the button for check balance. He waited. Again.

£30,134.70. How the hell had that happened? Hayden must have gasped.

'Problemo, head?' said Grego.

Hayden trembled with relief. His testicles relaxed. He pocketed his bank card, turned, and handed over the cash.

Grego Pope didn't bother counting it. He didn't need to. He got back in his cab and started the engine.[20] He wound the window down and gave Hayden a friendly wave. 'Thanks, pal. The wife'll be fucken deleerious.'

And off he rumbled to ruin someone else's life.

Hayden stared after the disappearing tail lights. Thirty thousand pounds in his account. That was a lot of money. There was only one way it could have got there. *Bad Blood*. With Julius Okeke on the case, Hayden had been paid for delivery of a working script! And that was merely the first instalment. He, Hayden McGlynn, had fed the beast. The beast was now feeding him.

Hayden felt a bit like Grego's wife. Think what he could do with thirty grand, not to mention all the future thirty grands, growing to three hundred grand then – why not? – three million, as his reputation grew! Dublin, London, Hollywood. A modest pad on Mauritius. Hold on. Forget modest. Forget Mauritius. Couldn't you buy your own island these days? Invite his new friends over to escape the hoi polloi, the hell of recognition. Grandiose plans, Hayden! Think huge! The universe is your oyster!

But whoa. What was all that stuff about wielding the sword of righteousness? Making a stand for his brethren and sisthren? Good question. But grass Wolfe up and destroy his own career? Hayden slowed down as he made his way past Old Joanna's and home. If he shopped Wolfe, the film would be put on hold. The project might be scrapped altogether. Where would that leave Hayden? His scriptwriting career in ruins. No agent. A pariah. No more thirty grands plus.

Hayden glanced at his watch. It was 2.31am. He wandered back through the empty streets and slipped his key, quietly, into Wolfe's front door.

\*

---

[20] Dark Cabs. *We undercut the undercutters.*

2.32. Hayden closed the door quietly. Wolfe Swift was still on the sofa, hunched over the laptop, Rusty nuzzling affectionately into his leg. Wolfe, lost to the world, his lupine eyes devouring the screen, its flickering images illuminating the brooding intensity of his handsome features. Apart from the light on the screen, all was dark. Hayden crept softly to the stairs, inched his way up and sat on the middle step, staring through the bannisters like a six-year-old. He could see the screen clearly over the top of Wolfe Swift's head. Even from the back, with no eyes to add to the mix, he oozed charisma. Not to mention tension. And no wonder; Wolfe Swift was watching the Oscars. The first screening since the ceremony switched to late October.[21]

This, for Wolfe, was a pivotal moment. If he was outed as the winner of best actress for *Invisible Woman*, it might destroy his career. Second if. Let's say it wasn't Wolfe, but let's further say that the actual winner decided to remain incognito. Wolfe would get the credit, Wolfe would get the blame. Take your pick. His career, the career of The Greatest Actor Of This Or Any Other Age, hung in the balance of public opinion. Big moment. No wonder he was perched on the edge of the sofa. No wonder he was temporarily out of character. Big moment for Hayden too. If Wolfe's cinema career was finished, so too was Hayden's. Back to the stand-up circle of hell. Back to a summer season supporting the Ukulele Orchestra of Largs. No wonder he was perched on the edge of the thirteenth step.

Hayden was mesmerised. On the screen, a podium. A speech. An envelope held aloft. One of Hollywood's finest saying something witty and amusing to camera, his teeth in the spotlight adding an extra glow to proceedings. The tone light but reverential.

The Hollywood luminary – perfect description given the teeth – opened the envelope. Took out the paper. Unfolded it.

---

[21] Following a request from the author of this book.* Such is the power of fiction.

* Plot continuity requirement.

Glanced at it impassively. Milked it. The coolest man on the planet. *He* knew. No-one else did. Then: 'And the winner for best actress is – Sherilee Lewis!'

Wolfe clenched a fist and punched the air. 'Huge fucking thank you, Sherry. Huge fucking thank you very much.'

He blew a kiss at the screen, which was suddenly lit up as a stunning black actress stood and approached the stage, smiling the width of the laptop. She looked absolutely radiant as she accepted the gold statuette. And she was so honored (sic) to accept the award, but she could never have done it without, oh her gosh, a huge, *huge* amount of help in winning this lil thang. 'God bless you Wolfe Swift. You were my inspiration. And God bless America.'

Hayden sat rooted to the step, negative thoughts about Wolfe now supplanted by the almost hypnotic need to watch as Wolfe leapt from the couch. The relief. The blessèd, blessèd relief. He played air guitar. The orgasmic release of that top F on the 22nd fret of the high E string. Legs splayed. Hayden stifled a laugh. Air guitar? Top F with splayed legs? What was the name of that group? The Fukwitz. *Too Fucked to Drink*. Wolfe was all three guitarists to the life.

As the imaginary Top F faded, Wolfe settled down. You can't top a top F. His whole body relaxed. He stood by the back window looking out at the dark, and sighed a contented sigh. Then? He buried his hands deep inside his jean pockets and rearranged his crotch. Back in character? Hayden again? Short answer: no, still Wolfe. It was a slightly different rearrangement. It added a humanity, a vulnerability, to this most intense and complex of men and suggested, subliminally, that Wolfe Swift was mightily relieved. The pressure was off. He could now get back to work. He rearranged his crotch again, this time Hayden-style. Hayden stifled another laugh. He still thought Wolfe was being Wolfe.

# 22

Hayden finally got to bed at 4.02. Within seconds he'd slipped into a deep and dream-filled sleep. Example: he dreamed of Herrs Freud and Jung entering the three aunts' boudoir, arguing furiously about the libido. *Mine is bigger than yours.* A quick glimpse of all three aunts in surgical stockings and little else but fortunately, at this point, the door slammed shut in his face. Ref. *The Annotated Hewbris* for full analysis.[22]

This segued neatly into a dream about his top E snapping as he approaches high F at Madison Square Gardens, which segued neatly into a dream of him lying half asleep in his childhood bedroom, perfect in every detail. He's about to stagger over to the window when he hears a plaintive, heartbreaking sound. It's him, Hayden McGlynn, sobbing uncontrollably. And then, as from afar, he hears himself as the small boy he once was, pleading with his Uncle Eddie:

*Why did Mammy and Daddy leave, Uncle Eddie? Did they – did they hate me?*

*Ah now, son.*

*But – I was only six.*

*Ah now to be fair, son, you were nearly seven. You were a big man, son, like your –*

*Like my – my daddy?*

---

[22] pp. 2304-31. *The Interpretation of Dreams Involving Sigmund Freud In A Personal Capacity* section.

*Like your – like your Uncle Eddie, son.*

*I wish you were my daddy, Uncle Eddie.*

*Ah now, son. Ah now. Run off and play like a good boy. That's – that's –*

Hayden sat up with a start. This was no dream. The voices were coming from the living room. This was beyond disturbing. Eddie? Eddie was dead. And Hayden? Hayden was a 43-year-old man. *He* was Hayden. He got out of bed and, without bothering to dress, made straight for the stairs. He stopped and looked over the bannisters in disbelief. There sat Wolfe at the writing desk, in character, hunched over Eddie's old tape machine. A coat tossed over Eddie's sofa showed where Wolfe had spent the night. His head was in his hands. The sound of weeping. Wolfe weeping. Eddie weeping. Hayden, as he continued his descent, almost weeping. The memories flooding back.

He was making his drowsy way to the kitchen, Rusty rubbing pathetically against his leg, when a loud rap on the front door jerked him fully awake. Hayden wiped a sleeve over his still-moist eyes, went over and opened up. The three aunts let themselves in, brushed past him as if he wasn't there, and surrounded the still weeping Wolfe.

'Will you look at yourself, Hayding.'

'What have we told you about listening to those tapes? You're a very bold boy, what are you?'

'He's a very bold boy, Florrie.'

'Dottie. And I was asking *him*. Sure *we* know that already.'

They tutted in mock-appalled unison.

'The *state* of this place.'

'Isn't it about time you settled down wit a lovely lady, Hayding, the way we can smell your undergarments from here.'

'Speaking of which, our next-door neighbour is perfect-amundo on the lovely lady front *we'd* say.'

'Beauuuutiful, Hayding. Really, really beauuuuutiful.'

'Not to mention a leading practitioner in the oldest profession, Hayding. Which is not the one you're tinking of, you bold boy you.'

'Did we tell you our teory on that one, Hayding? Only we've got dementia.'

'Did we tell you we've got dementia, only we don't know if we did or not on account of we've got dementia.'

'Or maybe we don't.'

'Now there's a ting. If we know we've got dementia that proves – by the very fact of knowing – that we *don't* have it.'

'Rejoice, Hayding.'

'We're cured!'

Hayden stood staring at them in slack-jawed disbelief. Rusty in London. The whole house, seemingly, a perfect match for Eddie's. And now this. His ancient, beloved aunts over from Dublin. Yet in surrounding Wolfe and giving him their full attention, they totally ignored *him*! It seemed Wolfe's Hayden act had fooled even his beloved aunts. Professor Emeritus Larry Stern was right again; the world was indeed a madhouse. Suddenly, as if to prove it, the three tiny aunts straightened their backs, lost a good sixty years and did a quick loosening up exercise in the middle of the floor. They looked straight at Hayden for the first time.

'There y'are, Haydo.'

'Isn't Wolfe gas, though?'

'I mean, Jesus! All this character immersion stuff is doing our nuts in.'

'If you want our opinion, he should try acting. It's a fuck of a lot easier.'

'Can't wait till we get to the actual shoot, though.'

'Three weeks till blast-off, Haydo.'

'He spurned our offer of a blow job. Something about incest.'

'Not that he was getting one anyway. Sure that sort of shags-for-parts codology went out weeks ago.'

They quick-marched to the still-open front door.

'Oh, and speaking of blow jobs, we'd put something on over those underpants.'

And off they hooted, leaving Hayden to pick up the inside of his head.

\*

Minutes after the Merrie Spinsters left, the two men sat facing each other. Wolfe, emotionally exhausted, cradling a bottle of *Sweet Ambrosia*. 'Sorry, man. It's just the way I am.' He stood up and took a quick swig. 'Plus, it gets worse. I've got to go *deep*.' He waved the bottle to illustrate his point. 'Backstory.' He shuddered and put the bottle down. 'I'm really putting you through it, yeah?'

Hayden grimaced. 'Honest answer?' he said, but before he could continue his eyes welled up.

Wolfe looked puzzled. 'What?'

Hayden shrugged.

'What? Tell me, man.'

'You... slept with Marina.' Hayden's voice broke. Wolfe went from puzzled to stunned. He stepped away and stared at Hayden.

'Did I?' He went from stunned to deeply troubled. 'Look,' he said, 'you do what the character tells you to do.' He moved over and put a brotherly arm around Hayden. 'It wasn't me, man. It was Hayden. That's –' he hesitated for a telling moment '– that's the beauty of acting, you know? It gets me away from –' Go on, Wolfe. Go *on*. All those years out of your life being someone else. Why do you do it? *Why?* 'It gets me away from myself. See, when I was little – sorry, man. You really don't want to know.'

He does, Wolfe. He *does*. What drives The Greatest Actor Of This Or Any Other Age? What makes him want to become someone else? He needs to know. The *reader* needs to know. *I* need to know. For fuck's sake, Hayden, *say* something.

'Go on.'

Wolfe composed himself, not acting now. Living. He snuffled and rewound. 'When I was little – hold on. Before I was little.

In the womb, yeh? Me. My twin brother. Well, he would have been my twin brother except he – except I –'

'Go on.'

Good man, Hayden. Softly spoken. Empathetic. Wolfe went on. 'He would have been born before me. My big brother, yeh? Except I – I wrapped the umbilical round his neck in a fit of –' Go on, Hayden. Tell him to go *on*. But Hayden didn't need to. Wolfe was compelled to unburden himself. 'Anyway, out I came. Couldn't look my mother in the eye. You know? So ever since, my whole life, I've been escaping – I've been escaping *me*.' I could dwell on this moving moment. The pain of it. The truth of it. The *poetry*. But, typical of this extraordinary artist, Wolfe Swift didn't. He snapped right out of it. Punched his palm for emphasis. 'Okay,' he said. 'Nothing is set in stone with this film yet, so maybe –' His voice trailed off.

Hayden waited. Nothing. 'Maybe what?' he said.

Wolfe shrugged. 'You know. It's a small budget movie. Cracking script. Could be a smash, but –' He took the bottle over to the kitchen, poured the contents down the sink, then stood with his back to Hayden, hands gripping the sink for support. 'Maybe I'm causing too much pain here. Maybe the movie's not worth it. You know? You. Marina. It wasn't me that – see? I can't even finish the sentence. But it wasn't me, it was you. Or maybe that's a story I tell myself.' He paused for a tragic moment. 'I feel terrible, man.' He gripped the sink tighter then, decision made, stood up straight. 'Tell you what. We could move on, okay? Cut the movie. Next project. Happens all the time.'

Hayden's life and career, his hopes, plans and dreams, his bank balance, his very essence as an adult human male, collapsed before him in a flash. He stared at the back of Wolfe's head – which may have had its own agenda – like a goldfish caught in headlights.

'Let me think about that,' he said.

*

Three weeks until filming started, the Merries had said. This cheered Hayden up. He could cope with that. Three more weeks, then Wolfe would be out on location. Working with other actors. Probably using the house for interiors, but otherwise off his case.

Hayden would be working on his next project. His career was back in the black. No venal ex-agent to hold him back. And maybe, looked at in the clear light of his bank balance, Wolfe *had* been Hayden at the time of the Marina debacle, so maybe it really was *Hayden* who had slept with Marina. Delusional? Arguably, but it worked. He'd seen the future, and the future was money. The future was success. The future was Hayden McGlynn. So all positive, for now at least, and if he could afford five hundred quid for a half-mile taxi ride, he could surely afford a modest makeover. He thought about a haircut but that reminded him of Lindsey, which further reminded him of DCI Pointer and murder, and he really didn't want to revisit all that. Think positive and the bad things go away.

Retail therapy. He pretended to be ironical about it, but that's what he did. Elvis Buthelezi jeans. Bull-skin biker jacket by Ruby Cohonez. Trainers by Sprung Rhythm. He even thought about a discreet man bag, but only because the three aunts had brought the subject up.

Shopping done, he dropped by Intersects, resplendent in his new outfit. He bought a coffee at the Browse & Quaff counter and found a comfy half-sofa. A mug-stained copy of *1,001 Movies You Gotta See Before I Kill You* by – who else? – Melanie 'Bud' Schultz, lay open on the table from the last customer. How's that for serendipity?

Hayden flicked through the book. Iconic movies, directors, actors. Here, for instance, are a couple of examples from Wolfe Swift's back catalogue: *Gran the Man*. Wolfe transitioned for this part, his manhood going on to separate success in *Fintan the Empathetic Penis*. They were subsequently reunited for *Confessions of a Justified Singer*, a biography of easy listening country crossover legend Pastor Enoch McCracken[23] whose catchphrase, 'Sex workers of Babylon!' endeared him to a younger generation of modish fundamentalists.

Now this, for Hayden, was deeply therapeutic. Wolfe had made dozens of films. He wouldn't be Hayden forever. Hayden started walking back to Wolfe's, snazzily dressed and reassuringly upbeat. A man with but a single goal: success! Wolfe, he reasoned, would move on to characters new. He, Hayden, would reclaim himself and also reclaim – his proprietorial word, not mine – Marina. Granted, that particular episode still hurt, but look at it this way: what would he have done if he'd been playing himself? He'd have done exactly as Wolfe had done. Which was exactly what Wolfe did.

He strolled along, physically and mentally upbeat. Strolled? Bounced! He was wearing his Sprung Rhythm trainers. Perfect. As he crossed over the canal at Kentish Town Road he tripped lightly past the mobile-in-the-water scene. The one physical link to his agent's untimely death. Hayden tosses Rich's mobile with the incriminating answerphone message on it into the canal, remember? Barge passes underneath.

Well, here's what happened: Vince Tupper of Barrow Boy Barges, a man of impeachable dishonesty, was showing a client the ropes, and happened to be passing under Kentish Town Road when a mobile phone landed on deck. He picked it up and chuckled wryly. His, he informed his startled female client, was bigger. Much, much bigger. He whipped it out of his chinos, which put her mind at rest in one way, and held both phones out. He was right. His *was* bigger. A lot bigger. His mobile rang. Important call – weren't they all? He took it and tossed Rich's mobile overboard, where it sank to the muddy bed and rested on the back-wheel spokes of a rusty bicycle. The barge moved slowly on.

---

[23] The Crooning Bigot.

Interesting fact: Vince was also the Vince Tupper of Barrow Boy Books and the Vince Tupper of DGM[24], arch-rival of Richard Mann's TLM. I mention this for my Buddhist readership of the forthcoming Burmese translation. It speaks of the interconnectedness of all things.

So. Retrospective stroke of luck for Hayden, and he didn't even know it. He was bouncing happily into the home stretch when a plainclothes cop car cruised past. He knew it was a cop car because he recognised, in the driver's seat, the huge, bulbous head of Detective Chief Inspector Ronnie Pointer. The car turned left onto Leverton Street, towards Wolfe's. Hayden felt his jaw clench. He thought of running back the way he'd come, but what good would that do? Pointer would track him down eventually and he'd have to face justice. British justice. As an Irishman, what chance did he have, especially taking his innocence into consideration? As far as the judicial system was concerned, that was a sure sign of guilt. He turned onto Leverton Street, but then stooped behind an upright bin with a good vantage point and waited, his imagination on overdrive. The knock on the door. The no answer. The call for reinforcements round the back – with marksmen. Bit dramatic? It was the paranoia thinking.

What happened next, however, threw him. He peeked round the side of the bin. The police car was double-parked. DCI Pointer got out and had a quick look at the house numbers. He was about to amble up to the wrong door when it opened and hugely successful comedian Little Jimmy Lawrie came out, hands raised in it's-a-fair-cop-guv mode.

Little Jimmy a suspect? Now there was a twist. But why would Little Jimmy want to kill Rich? It didn't make sense. Moneywise, he was way out of Rich's league. Hayden crouched closer to listen in. Pointer opened the cop car door gracefully, a man in control of his own narrative, and eased Little Jimmy down. The way they do. Guiding hand on the head. As Little

---

[24] Dodgy Geezer Management

Jimmy bent to car level, Pointer talked him through it. The way they also do.

'Murder is my game, Mr Lawrie, not tax evasion. And no doubt you could have made your own way to the station for a little chat, but I'm retiring soon, and the lads thought why not? Old Ronnie? Big fan of the comedy genre. Let's give him this one. Parting gift type thing. Ah. Speaking of which.' He reached in to the dashboard. 'Brought a copy of your book along if you wouldn't mind signing. Christmas present for the lady wife sorted. Anyway. I expect you'll get plenty more material where you're headed.'

He slid Little Jimmy into the car and produced a pair of handcuffs from his coat. He dangled them playfully for effect, but Hayden was tucked away behind the bin and there was no-one else there. Pointer shrugged philosophically, got back into the car and closed the door. As he did so, Wolfe sped along the pavement ranting into a mobile. Hayden froze. He was living out the incriminating phone call, the one he insisted take place in bed with Marina. So why do it in full view of the public, and why now? Whatever the reason – a line run-through? – his version of Hayden, the voice, the body language, the rage as he threatens to kill Rich, was perfect in every detail.

*'Just a quickie, Dickie. Can't do the tour.'*

PAUSE.

*'Well, Dickie, it's like this. Too fucking busy. Wolfe Swift, Rich. Heard of him? Irish 'fillum' actor. Six Oscars. Wants to shoot my script.'*

PAUSE.

*'We? Nah, Dickie. Here's how I play it. First fillum,* Bad Blood. *Not about us, Dickie, so relax. For now. Follow up.* Rich Mann, Dead Mann. *He kills his agent. That's you, Rich.'*

Pointer was about to start the engine when he spotted Wolfe in the rear-view mirror. He wound down the window as an incandescent Wolfe reached the house. Ranting.

*'No idea how to do it yet, but don't worry, pal. Hate will find a way.'*

Pointer smiled knowingly. 'Don't tell me, Pat,' he said. 'Dodgy client, is it? Unpaid bill?' He winked at Wolfe. 'Still, can't stand around chatting all day. Catch you later, eh?'

Wolfe glowered at him and went inside. Pointer wound the window up and drove off. Hayden shifted his weight from one leg to the other. He stayed crouching behind the bin for some time, palpitating. *Catch you later, eh? Did Pointer mean that literally?* Hayden was pretty sure he did. He wound back through their several chance encounters. Pointer coming back to Snip Snip for his gloves. It certainly seemed suspicious at the time. Pointer in Dublin for the golf. Maybe that wasn't so innocent after all. Oh, and Pointer outside Old Joanna's taking notes. Why? Why would a detective chief inspector of the London Met take down the names of comedians if he wasn't onto something? And now, Little Jimmy Lawrie living conveniently nearby. Pointer, he feared, was closing in on his innocence and nothing, but nothing, was going to get in his way.

Hayden stood up, creaking, and was trying to reintroduce his knees to the standing position when his mobile rang. Julius Okeke. 'You have received a large sum of money, my friend. The goat is on life support.' End call.

*The goat is on life support.* Hayden winced. The goat wasn't the only thing. He was on life support, and there was only one route out of his predicament.

Locate the perp.

Close the case.

Feed the beast.

And there was one person who knew more than he was letting on.

# 23

Lindsey was about to close up. Even from a distance he looked terrible. As soon as he spotted Hayden walking towards Snip Snip he waved at him to get a move on, ushered him in and double-locked the door. He wrapped a cape around a startled Hayden and motioned him to the hair chair. Sit. Hayden sat. Lindsey went over to the window and yanked at the blind. It got stuck lop-sided and half-way. He yanked again, nothing, came back trembling and grabbed the back of the chair.

'And what would Sir – no, sorry. Displacement activity. Stop it, Lindsey!' He paused. Deep breath. 'Start again. So, I went to my analysts but I can't remember a thing about it. I keep getting flashbacks to three tiny little voices talking about – stop it, Lindsey. Thing is, I'm starting to disintegrate, and it's all because of – Oh, Rich! Rich! Why? *Why?*' He pulled the cape tight around Hayden's neck. 'Look, I admit I left poor Richard in a panic. I mean, I couldn't tell Pointer *that*. But I didn't do it, as God is my witness. Do you believe in God, by the way? Me neither. Some witness. But I didn't do it. Whoever came in, well, all they had to do –'

Lindsey stopped suddenly. Hayden could sense him starting to sob. They made eye contact in the mirror. 'Tell you what,' Hayden said, 'why don't you give me the lightest of light trims while you're at it and tell me everything you know about Rich's sad demise. From the beginning.'

Lindsey grabbed his scissors like a comfort blanket. 'Really? Oh, *bless* you. That would be *so* therap*eutic*.'

Hayden's hair was the right length as it was, but a trim would be worth it if he got to the bottom of this whole sorry mess. Or maybe not. The scissors twitched in Lindsey's hands. Snip snip. Snip snip snip.

'Okay,' said Hayden, 'you left Richard in a panic. Where?'

'What? Oh, upstairs,' said Lindsey. 'He indulged in a little, shall we say peccadillo. He was a control freak, see? Loved nothing more than tying people up, contractually speaking, and watching them squirm. Oh, the stories he told me. Let me see. Hayden – Hayden –'

'McGlynn,' said Hayden.

'Ah yes. Of course. He told me all about *you*.' He smiled at Hayden but his eyes, in the mirror, had a troubled look. 'Hot shave while we're at it? Oh, goody. Kettle's boiled. Yes, he had this sort of running joke about sending you to Largs. But as Rich always said, you don't manipulate others without paying a price, so he liked to relax –' Lindsey leaned in so close Hayden could feel his breath against his ear '– by manipulating *himself*. It's an auto-erotic thing. You know? All noosed up.' There was a silence as Lindsey slopped boiling water into a bowl and placed a trembling cut-throat on the counter. 'I used to keep an eye on things, so to speak,' he continued, 'in case it all went horribly wrong. Not really my thing if I'm honest, but I think it gave him an added kick, plus, okay, it paid well. Anyway, all he had to do was utter his safe word and I'd *jerk his noose*. Back to planet earth. Except this particular time someone was buzzing up. Door was locked, of course, for privacy. Except this person must have known the code. "One two three four, Linz. Who's going to think of *that?*" Well *someone* did. Anyway, next thing I knew I heard a very, very angry voice coming up the stairs.' He squirted shaving foam on Hayden's chin, smoothed it roughly over his neck and cheeks, and rattled the cut-throat in the mug. 'Where was I? Oh yes.' His voice rose several decibels. '"Rich *bleep* Mann, you *bleeping bleeping bleep*!"'

The cut-throat throbbed in his white-knuckled hand.

'Tell you what,' said Hayden. 'Maybe –'

But Lindsey was on transmit, not receive. His eyes, in the mirror, looked borderline psychotic. He sliced the razor through the air to illustrate his point. '"I'm going to *bleep* you, you *bleeping bleeper*!" There I was and there was Rich. Heavy steps coming up the stairs. I mean it could have been anyone! So I panicked, didn't I? Climbed out the window, onto the fire escape and down. Next thing I knew, those old fools were trying to rewrite my sign *again* and I forgot all about Rich. Until –' Lindsey lowered the razor to Hayden's neck with a quivering hand, overcome with emotion. 'I mean, I should've stayed and looked after him, but I'm a one-man man, you know? If my husband got to hear I was helping Rich... I mean, what was I *thinking*? So I ran.' He tilted Hayden's head to one side with his free hand and drew the razor across his terrified skin. 'Besides, whoever was coming up the stairs, I thought it was all bluster, you know? People are always angry with Rich for some reason or other. Up they'd come, undo the rope, give the kinky sod what for. But they didn't. Why? *Why?*'

Lindsey was about to run the razor across his Adam's apple, when Hayden spotted Lenny Broonstein slinking past on the other side of the road. Hands deep in pockets, head bowed, like a man with a guilty conscience. Of course! Lenny *'Ah Hate Everything'* Broonstein! Why hadn't he thought of it before? Lenny was a stand-up. Rich was Lenny's agent. Hayden had seen his contract. *All tied up?* It gave him a motive, and Lenny certainly had the temperament for murder. Hayden lifted the cape with a discreet movement of the wrist and pushed the razor delicately away, as if defusing a bomb. The cut-throat trembled in Lindsey's trembling hand.

'The intruder,' said Hayden. 'Did he sound anything like this? *Ah hate black people! White people! People wi' wee pink spotties!*'

Hayden's Glasgow sounded more like Ballymena, but he got the rage bit right. It had a curiously calming effect on Lindsey, as if the pent-up fury had passed from one body to another. 'Come to think of it,' he said, 'he did sound a bit – Celtic.' He was about to get back to business with the cut-throat, but Hayden slid out of the chair, pulled the cape off and made for the door.

'Looks triff,' he lied, not glancing in the mirror. 'Stick it on my account.'

\*

Minutes later he was in hot pursuit down Kentish Town Road. 'Oi! Lenny!'

No answer. Lenny slunk faster. Hayden shouted again. Lenny slunk faster still. One more try. Lenny disappeared down a side street. As Hayden strode briskly along in pursuit of his prime suspect, because that's what Lenny now was, he ran over in his mind what he could remember of *Lenny Broonstein's Rant*, aka *Ah Hate*.

Hayden could pretty well repeat it from memory. He did so, mostly to himself, but the odd line escaped into the outside world as he got into the manic swing. *Irish cunts, English cunts, cunts from anywhere cunts*, for instance. That line popped out unbidden. One or two interesting responses from passers-by, but we won't dwell on them. Besides, this was Kentish Town Road. You expected such things, often with a passable Glaswegian accent. Worth pointing out here that Hayden's lower face was still coated in shaving foam, which may have added to the psychotic effect.

*Rich cunts, cunts called Rich.* Ah. That was the line he was after. Hayden tried calling again. 'Cunt!' Whoops. He'd slipped into character a bit too skilfully. Lenny walked faster, a sure sign of guilt. He arrived at a high-rise block of flats and rooted frantically for his key. This was getting more and more interesting. Hayden was pumping adrenalin. He could get used to this. He broke into a run, but before he could catch up Lenny had slipped inside and, seconds before Hayden got to it, the main door clicked shut.

Hayden stared through the grubby glass panel as Lenny disappeared into the lift. He was about to turn away when he clocked the shaving foam and wiped it off with his sleeve. Then he examined the buzzers. A lot of floors, a lot of names. Wonderfully multi-cultural, reflecting the diversity at the heart of this great city. O'Toole, Ranjitsinhji, Bruce. Ayoade, Persondottir, Smith. Seventeenth floor, Broonstein. Had to be worth a shot. He pressed the buzzer. Long pause, then 'Hello?' A tentative hello. An expecting-trouble hello.

'Hello yourself,' said Hayden. 'I'm looking for Lenny.'

'Oh dear,' said the voice. Small, frail, identifiably female.

'It's all right,' said Hayden. 'Name's Hayden. We're pals.'

'Leonard has a friend?' The voice sounded stronger, as if it had taken succour from this simple line. 'That's lovely, dear, but I'm afraid Leonard isn't here at the moment.'

'Trust me,' said Hayden. 'By the time I get up to the seventeenth floor he will be.'

'Well in that case, dear –'

The buzzer buzzed. Hayden pushed the door. He was in. He pressed the button for the lift. He waited. It came. He got in. It went up as requested. Seventeenth floor. He got out. He looked for the door marked Broonstein. He found it. He pressed yet another buzzer. From inside, as he waited, he heard what sounded to Hayden like an electric wheelchair whining over a parquet floor. The door opened. Woman in electric wheelchair. Parquet floor. 'Ah, hello,' he said. 'You must be Lenny's sister.'

Old trick this. It wouldn't work if it *was* his sister. No. Has to be the mother. I've used it myself to great effect, though once it worked to my disadvantage. An old acquaintance. Let's call him Declan. His grandmother – in this case – was smitten. I ended up in a six-month one-sided relationship. Couldn't shake the woman off. She eventually died and, sore point, left me nothing. But that was me and then. This is Hayden and now.

Lenny's mother blushed prettily. 'Oh you,' she said. 'Sister indeed. But do come in.' She steered the wheelchair around.

'Mazel tov, Leonard! You have a friend. A mother's prayers answered. Thank you, Yahweh, thank you.'

See what I mean? Multi-cultural. Possibly Welsh.

She led the way into the living room. 'Le – where *is* that boy? He's a good boy, Hayden. But shy? Don't talk to me about shy. Leonard!' She turned to Hayden. 'Go into his bedroom, dear. He's got to Palestine on his peace quilt. Such concentration as I have never seen in a quilter. But go. Go. Leonard!'

Hayden went. He didn't have to look for the door. It had Lenny's name on it. *Leonard's Room.* Hayden knocked politely.

'Push. Push. He's not used to people. Push.' Then, quietly but passionately to herself, 'Freyen zikh! A friend!'

Hayden pushed. He went in. Lenny was lost in his quilt work. Fascinating from a political perspective. I won't describe it in detail, because one man's peace is another woman's war – and besides, I don't want to alienate my more bigoted readers – but it was an indescribably beautiful piece of work and suggested that Lenny Broonstein, in the privacy of his bedroom at least, was a bit of a revelation if all you knew of him was the stage version. Lenny turned to face Hayden, his eyes, close up, betraying a vulnerable and, yes, pleading look.

'You won't tell anyone, will you?' he said.

And Hayden, to his credit, never did. He left Lenny's with a new and deeper understanding of the unfathomable complexity of the human psyche. And a salt beef bagel. Oh, and Lenny was innocent. No question. A peace quilter like that? Murder? It was unthinkable.

So, guilt yes, because Lenny was riven with guilt, but as I suspected, the wrong kind of guilt.

Welsh guilt.

# 24

Back home, Wolfe Swift had taken character immersion to a new level. His work on backstory involved striding around the living room, clutching a bottle of Uncle Eddie's *Sweet Ambrosia* with a frightening intensity that both appalled and fascinated Hayden. Was Hayden really like that in his, thus far, darkest hour? Pretty impressive if he was, but in the here and now Wolfe and his fervid alter-ego were, to put it politely, upsetting Hayden's mental equilibrium.

He couldn't wait for night to roll around, and when it did he headed straight to Old Joanna's for a quick word with Steve. If Lindsey was to be believed, Rich had been murdered by a client with a grievance. Hayden, for instance. Except it wasn't Hayden. Hayden knew that. It was hardly Lenny either. Lenny's comic persona was mad-rant rage. In person, however, he was a gentle peace-quilter. So, not Hayden, not Lenny. Who then? Steve knew everybody. He'd help Hayden tick off the probables, the possiblies, the couldn't-possiblies and so on. At least it would narrow the field. He left a confused-looking Rusty alone in the house with Wolfe; all this two-Haydens business was pretty confusing for a dog.

Hayden also had to deal with the mental fallout from a double dose of himself, but this he could deal with. Two more weeks. Shoot. Wolfe off the case. Back to the status quo. One Hayden at a time he could deal with. One anybody, come to that, which is what greeted him in Old Joanna's. Baldy, singular, sat at his usual place at the corner of the bar. Staring into his empty glass. Dreaming of the glory days. The birth of comedy. Hayden grabbed a stool.

Steve screwed the lid off a sparkling water and placed it on a beer mat. A glass with ice and lemon, another beer mat. No alcohol, two beer mats. Public house terminology doesn't cater for teetotal. Not that this exercised Steve. He accepted the world the way it was. One exception. You could never over-polish your counter. 'Here for our mutual friend's farewell?' he said. 'Thought you'd steer well clear, to be honest.'

'Our mutual friend?' said Hayden. 'Which particular one are we talking about?'

'Boy Wonder himself,' said Steve. 'Foetus O'F.'

'Foetus? Farewell? Why? Where's he headed?'

'The Shores of Amerikay quote unquote,' said Steve. 'New management, apparently. The lad's back on form. As you can probably hear.'

The roar from The Woom confirmed this. Hayden kept his own counsel. He wasn't going to be drawn into anything that might be misunderstood as flattery.

He cradled his glass as Steve pulled a pint. There was no doubt about it. Foetus was getting a response far greater than his modest talent deserved. But that's the typical audience for you. You can't force people to have taste beyond their abilities. According to Stern, most people are stuck on Comedy Levels One and Two. If you're still reading this, you're on Four – at least! – so relax. Besides, we mustn't denigrate the lower levels. They could be members of your own family. Having said that, it does get a bit dispiriting at times. But there. I've said my piece. It's not, as I say, about you. It's about them. Now read on.

Wild applause and manic whoops announced the first encore. This grated with Hayden, but Baldy Mayle stared into his empty glass, oblivious. 'I invented comedy, me,' he said.

'Try telling that to Aristophanes,' muttered Hayden.

It hadn't been meant for public consumption, but Baldy's comic antennae picked it up. 'Greek basted,' he sneered. 'Just cos he got there ferst.'

By this stage a few comedians had dropped by from other venues and were busy outdoing each other in quips and drolleries at the bar. Hayden, pretending to be lost in his own thoughts, listened in and watched with the detached eye of the seasoned sleuth. It could be any of them, he thought. He needed information on each and every one. Professional relationship to the deceased, for example. Degree to which they blamed Rich for their own lack of talent and so on. All of which could take some time. He began ticking off the definitely-nots. Several, for instance, were with Vince Tupper at DGM. Vince was a dodgy geezer, but you were supposed to think he wasn't because he called his outfit Dodgy Geezer Management. This was post-irony, but Dodgy Geezer himself didn't know that. His acts were Level One. Go with the money. And male. Go with what you know. On the plus side, however, he wasn't Richard Mann.

The door opened. The whoops and hollers subsided. The audience poured out and into the bar. Hundreds of them. Well, however many the place held. The heat of the room came out with them, and with the heat came Detective Chief Inspector Ronnie Pointer. Hayden's heart walloped against his ribcage. *Catch you later, eh?* This was later and, as if it was all preordained, Pointer headed straight over to him, a bland expression on his face. An expression that gave nothing away. Clever. Very, very clever. Or maybe just bland. Impossible to tell. Which made it, possibly, even more clever. 'You again, Pat. Night off, is it? Comedy fan, are we?'

'Ehh,' said Hayden. 'Yes. Big fan. Big fan.'

'Magic. Me too. Bit of a break from the day job. Murder with me, Pat, painting with you. Not to mention decorating.'

Hayden wasn't sure where he was going with this, but he didn't like it. Not one bit. Was there a mocking undertone? Did he know more than he was letting on?

'Couldn't get in?' said Pointer, jerking his head towards The Woom.

'N-no,' said Hayden. 'He's a pretty popular guy.'

'That he is, my son. That he is. *Hey fella, where you from?! Termonfeckin!* Now you.'

Hayden gritted his teeth. '*Yow.*'

Detective Chief Inspector Pointer smiled encouragingly. 'Can't hear you.'

Hayden clenched his face.

'*Yow!*'

It came out louder than expected. With venom.

'Magic,' said Pointer. 'And here's the man himself.' He winked at Hayden. 'Watch this. Little party trick.'

Foetus emerged from The Woom and was immediately surrounded by Level Twos. *Termonfeckin*ing. *Yow*ing. Immortalising themselves in selfies with their doe-eyed hero, who stood courting flattery as if he deserved it. Pointer ambled over and placed a practised hand on Foetus' shoulder. 'Detective Chief Inspector Ronnie Pointer of the Met,' he proclaimed. 'Consider yourself well and truly nicked.'

If Foetus hadn't been surrounded by well-wishers he would have collapsed with fright.

'*Nnng?*' he said. Difficult to illustrate in writing the fear in that *nnng*, the panic behind his one visible eye.

Pointer chortled jovially. 'Relax, my son. Little bit of harmless joshing. Big fan. Big fan.' He punched Foetus playfully on the arm. '*Termonfeckin!*'

Foetus gulped like a timorous frog. '*Yow.*' A weak yow. A feeble yow. Not the yow of a Boy Wonder about to make it Big. As he autographed Pointer's charge sheet with a shaking hand, Hayden gave him the cold, clinical stare of the seasoned sleuth.

\*

The fuss had died down. The Level Twos had dispersed. Pointer had gone home 'to report back to the lady wife.' Baldy was sorting out the comedy pecking order. Baldy. Aristophanes. Everyone else. In that order. He smiled happily into his empty glass. History, after all, is what you make it.

Foetus, now fully recovered, stood at the bar. Still courting flattery, but largely ignored by his fellow professionals, who were busy courting flattery themselves. Except that *they* weren't hot. *They* weren't about to go to Amerikay. *They* hadn't got three encores.

Hayden, now in sleuth mode, saw an opening. 'Top up for my friend here when you're ready, Steve.' Foetus looked confused. Friend? Me? Hayden pressed home his advantage. 'As I was saying to the estimable DCI Pointer,' – he gritted his teeth again – 'big fan, big fan.'

Foetus stared at him. 'Really? You're joking me, right?'

'I'm a comedian,' said Hayden. 'Comedy is my life. But I hope' – calculated pause through gritted teeth[25] – 'I hope I'm allowed to admire exceptional talent.'

'Really?'

Slightly higher pitch this time. Hayden's apparent magnanimity broke all the first rules of comedy. He leaned closer still. 'Strictly *entre nous*,' he said. 'My film script. You know. The one with Wolfe. Sorry. First name terms.'

'You're making a movie with Wolfe Swift?' Foetus was about to say *really?* again. Hayden overrode it. 'You hadn't heard?'

'Well, yeah,' said Foetus, 'course I heard. I just thought, you know –'

Hayden knew. He overrode that too. 'Main character? Slightly younger H. McGlynn. Script done and dusted. Few minor changes. Shoot imminent. Fame guaranteed.' He put a hand on Foetus' shoulder. 'That come-back-when-you're-born-you-can-play-the-afterbirth crack a while back. Low blow. But bear with me. I checked out your DVD.'

'What? *Foetus First?*'

---

[25] Comedy is easy, flattery is hard.

Phew. Thanks for the title, Foet. 'The very same.' As if on cue, a text pinged in. Hayden glanced at his mobile. Excellent. He chuckled wryly. 'Agents,' he said. 'What are they like?' He shoved the phone at Foetus.

*beast comatose do I make myself clear*

'Julius Okeke. What can I say?'

He could see Foetus was impressed. He sent a quick response – *Im on it* – and turned back to a wide-eyed, salivating Foetus. 'Thing is, and this is strictly *entre nous*,' – he leaned super-conspiratorially over – 'you'd be better than Wolfe for the part.'

Third *Really?*. Falsetto.

'Totally,' said Hayden. 'You literally burn through the screen. So does Wolfe, no question. Big difference, though. You've got that comedy thing, you know? That *je ne sais quoi*? It's in the genes.' He almost added that Foetus would have made a brilliant Invisible Woman, but stopped himself in time. Don't blow it with hyperbole. 'Goes without saying you'd have to audition.' He lowered his voice. 'One word. Technicality.'

Foetus looked puzzled. 'But – Wolfe Swift is never going to drop out. Is he?'

Good question. Hayden had thought of that. 'Here's the plan,' he said. 'I'll undermine him. Work away at his self-belief. Never fails.' He paused for the punchline. 'An actor playing a comedian? They never get it right.'

Foetus thought about this. 'You're right,' he said. 'They never do.'

Hayden smirked inwardly. 'So, maybe we should meet up,' he said. 'Quick drink, you know? You could do a bit of Haydenwatching when I'm not looking. Check out my mannerisms. Get inside the character, so to speak.'

Foetus nodded slowly. He was on it already. There was this thing Hayden did with his trousers. He'd build that in. Not now, though. Hayden was off again.

'But first? The aforementioned drink. How's that sound?'

Foetus grinned the manic grin of the ego unleashed. Better than Wolfe Swift? Hoh?

'Game ball,' he pretty well yelped.

'Game ball indeed,' said Hayden.

Whatever *that* meant.

# 25

'A blank page is an idea waiting to happen.'

*Han Sung Yee*

Hayden sat at his desk, sifting through old ideas. Feed the beast.[26] He felt positive, murder case in hand, *Bad Blood* on its way – but there was still the small matter of that all-important follow-up script. *Bad Blood* had been pretty straightforward. Lifted from life itself. But how often can you do that? In Hayden's case, once. He needed to capitalise on his big break, and his notebooks, filled with gags and five-minute riffs, yielded nothing.

Outside, the sound of fireworks. It was that time of year again. Bang! He was about to go out and walk himself into an idea – catch himself by surprise, so to speak – when his mobile rang. He reached out to take the call – but hold on. What if it was Julius? What if it was the police? He didn't have a new project for Julius. He didn't want to help Pointer with his enquiries. On the other hand, he couldn't keep ignoring his phone. He glanced at the screen. Number unknown. Oh, what the hell.

'Yes?'

---

[26] Ref. *Julius Okeke's Goat.* Inspirational Reith lecture by the legendary talent agent.

'Hi. Hayden?'

Not Julius. Not Pointer. Good start.

'Got it in one,' he said. 'Sorry, who is this?'

'*Guardian*,' said the voice. Hayden sat up. 'We're planning a feature on comedy roots. Word has it you're involved in a project with Wolfe Swift, and we wondered if you'd be interested in taking part.'

Hayden relaxed on his chair. Foot on the desk relaxed. He'd have to get used to this. Might as well start now. 'Shoot,' he said.

'Now? Great! Okay. Question one: influences.'

'Well,' drawled Hayden, 'Good question. I'd have to say I've probably influenced quite a few people over the years. Lemme think.' Hayden didn't have to think. He knew what he was going to say. 'I see young Foetus O'Flaherty has tried stealing some of my comedic clothes, so to speak. Nothing I can do about that. They look up to you at that age, I suppose –'

'Ah, sorry, I was actually talking about the other way round. Who's influenced *you*?'

'Oh. Right. Well now. Let me see.' Hayden was obviously thrown by the question. 'I suppose you could say I've been influenced by great writers through the ages, although one doesn't wish to sound pompous.'

'I was thinking more, like, comedians?'

'You know something?' said Hayden. 'That's a very challenging question, because I don't think I've ever been influenced by another comedian *per se*. My influences have been more, shall we say, literary.'

If I might butt in here – come *on*. I may have touched on this before, but Hayden used to watch *me* when he was starting out. The mike stance. The laconic delivery. The more-shall-we-say-literary influences. All mine. *Per* fucking *se*. And another thing, while we're on the subject; take Hayden's Jewish gag. Pretty good as Jewish gags go, but who got there first with the convinced-I-was-Jewish schtick? I don't think I need to answer that one. Take a break. Check it out on the internet. I'll wait.

\*

\*

What can I say? Referenced in Stern's *Genesis of the Gentile Jewish Joke*[27] at Level Five. Hayden's? Not so good. But good. Level Three. Maybe Four. Five? *Get outta here!*

I didn't catch the rest of his conversation with the *Guardian* journalist. There were lots of fireworks going off outside – *Bang!* – interspersed with Hayden-waffle about Samuel bloody Beckett, who would never have lasted five minutes on a Friday night at the Glasgow Empire. Particularly his later stuff.

Positively preening, Hayden put the mobile down. I was a bit disappointed in him. But what can you do? Nothing. Hayden, on the other hand, can compound the problem, and this he did in a way that still stuns me whenever I think about it. He opened his laptop. He opened a new word document. He wrote a single word. *Title*. He added a colon. Intriguing. He hadn't gone beyond the preen. No hint of self-doubt. He'd found his big idea.

---

[27] *aka Heard The One About The Gentile Jew?*

He put the kettle on, whistling happily to himself, and returned to the laptop. He typed another single word. *Ravishing*. He started to type a manic synopsis, speeding up as the ideas flooded out.

*My* title.

*My* ideas.

I couldn't believe it. Yet I believed it.

Because everything he wrote – every character, every plot twist, every scene – was mine.

\*

If you dislike puns as much as I do,[28] you might want to skip the next paragraph.

Hayden arranged to meet Foetus at 'the drinkerie of your choice. On me.' Foetus chose *Híbín*. Bear with me. *Síbín* is Gaelic for illicit drinkerie. *Síbín*? *Híbín*? She Been He Been. Get it? 'Thought I'd reclaim the word for the lads,' quipped restaurateur and media celebrity Kerry McRoom. 'Sure don't the feckin ladies *run* the world these days?' Sides split yet? Now read on.

*Híbín* is set deep in the heart of merry London. A badly lit cellar with rickety tables, a jumble of seats that probably came off a skip, and that type of spiritually charged folk-rock-punk that gives the Irish a bad name the world over.

Luckily for Hayden, Foetus was already well oiled when he got there. Move to the States? Better than Wolfe? He was on a well-deserved alcohol-fuelled high. His one eye open to the public was glazed, his forelock already at that stage where it kissed the lip of his drink. Perfect. Hayden could use that. All he had to do now was reel him in. He ordered two plates of the chef's special: Irish stew. 'And a bottle of your finest house red. Oh, and open another bottle, garçon. Let it breathe.' The waiter gave him a filthy look and whipped the menus away.

---

[28] As does Stern. Ref. his pithy rant, *Sarcasm: The Second Lowest Form of Wit*.

Drinks served, Hayden managed a quick 'Lash into that, Foet. Remember, you're drinking for both of us.' The rest was a Foetus O'Flaherty monologue, soundtracked by the fireworks still going off outside. Hopes. Dreams. Brilliant career to date. *Bang!* Always knew he'd be big. But as big as he was going to be? He didn't know that level of big even *existed*, for fuck's sake. But he was up for it. *Bang!* He'd started on the second bottle when the sullen waiter came over.

'Everything okay?' he muttered. Solicitous. It was part of the job.

'Love the stew,' said Hayden. 'Did you open the tin yourself?'

The waiter wanted to kill him. But he didn't. 'That's a good one alright,' he sneered, and kicked Hayden to death down a back alley in his head.

Fortunately for Hayden he was about to go off duty. His replacement was an ebullient Australian waitress who came straight over. 'Everything okay, guys?' Solicitous. It was part of her personality.

Foetus gave her his best lopsided smile. Cutesy. Little Boy Lostish. Drunk. 'Love the stew,' he slurred. 'Did you open the tin yourself?'

The Australian waitress hooted. 'Oh my *gosh*,' she gushed. 'That is *so funny*. Hey. Aren't you…? Oh *wow*. Foetus O'*Flah*erty! You are so *sexy*. You have simply *got* to do a tour down under.'

Hayden glowered at her. He knew what was coming. And here it came. 'I'd be happy to do a tour of your down under any time.'

'Oh *wow*. You are so, so *funny*.' A hand gesture of mock shock. Foetus could do no wrong. 'Whoops. Gotta go. Other tables.' She turned and addressed the room. 'Hey guys. Foetus O'Flaherty. *Did you open the tin yourself?* Top gag!'

Hayden was discreetly seething. He had to keep a tight rein on his emotions if he wanted to achieve the desired result. And now was the time to pounce. Foetus was sitting up in his chair, simpering modestly and pretending to examine his phone. Let my people stare. Hayden took his own mobile out. There was a small window of opportunity between drunk and comatose. The window was open for business. He placed his mobile surreptitiously on the table, pressed record, and dived in.

'You must have been a bit upset when old Rich died,' he said.

Foetus was lost to the world on a pink cloud of ego. Foetus O'Flaherty. Yes, I am he. *Wham!* The 'Rich' word suddenly registered. He forgot about his mobile and focused, momentarily, on Hayden. 'Are you joking me or what? The guy was a total arse. Had me booked for a summer season in fucking *Cleethorpes*. So when I got this offer Stateside – new management, the works – I phoned Rich Cunt – that's what I called him, Rich Cunt – and he says, "No can do, little Foety," – something about triple lock management, lifetime contracts – "So what are you going to do?" he says, "kill me?" Well, let's say I got a bit upset. "Diddums," says Mister Triple Fucking Lock. I was furious. Diddums yourself you scheming shit cunt bastard.'

Foetus was peaking too early. Hayden slowly topped his glass up as Foetus, visible eyelid drooping, swayed gently at the other side of the table. Hayden waited till he'd gulped down half his glass. Now was the time for the coup de grâce. The masterstroke. Hayden leaned across the table, placed a hand over his mobile to muffle the recording and dropped his voice to the level of boastful intimacy. 'Of course, you realize *I* killed him.'

Foetus stared at him. The I-cannot-be*lieve*-you-*said*-that stare. He was so exercised by the bald effrontery of the statement that he almost sobered up. 'That, my friend,' he slurred, 'is where you are one thousand per cent wrong.'

Hayden held his gaze steadily. 'Is that so?' He paused for maximum effect. 'Go on then. Prove it.' Hayden leaned back but kept eye contact.

'Okay,' said Foetus. 'I will.' Hayden took his hand discreetly off his mobile. Foetus leaned in. 'So, like, metaphorically speaking, there's me in one corner, there's Rich in the other. Whatsit force, removable object.' Hayden willed him on. Less of the waffly intro. 'Okay. Series of texts. Fuck you. No, fuck you. No, fuck *you*. I'm paraphrasing, right? Back and forth, back and forth, back and forth. No shift in his position, so I decide to drop round. Buzz up. No answer. Again. No answer. Fair enough. Except he told me the door code when he took me on. "One two three four, Foet. Who's going to think of that, eh?" One two three four click. I'm in. Up the stairs. Ranting. "I want out, Rich. Compren?"

'Into the office. There's this other guy vamoosing out the window. And there's Rich in the side room. All tied up! Leather pouch thing. Head in a noose. Dancing a jig on a stool. And there's me putting it to him in plain English. "I signed that contract in good faith, Rich, blah-de-blah!" Cunt keeps croaking "Abort! Abort!" I'm thinking fuck you. Foetus is not my real fucking name. My real name is Fergus. And the face on him! He's like a beetroot on the booze. Well, I'm sort of single-mindedly pursuing my contractual freedom issues at this point so I think he's being, like, intransigent. "Will you fucking stop saying fucking abort," I say. "And lay off with the fucking jig."'

He gazed blearily over at Hayden. Hayden gave him the hard stare. Come on. Come *on*. Before you flop over.

'So, where was I? Right, yeh. I kick the chair away. I'm fucking angry, you know? Not thinking, like. Anyway, he lets out a sort of strangulated whine. "It's my safe word, Foet. Abor-r-r-r-t!"' Foetus took a quick slurp from his glass. 'Then I remember. The guy out the window. Course it all makes perfect sense then. Safe word. Window guy is supposed to, like, abort. "Well," I say, "fair enough, I feel your pain and shit, but I'd like you to sign a desideratum first. A sine qua non, if you will. If that's not, like, too much trouble. Then I'll sort you out and we can all get on with our lives."'

Hayden sat back. Latin? Foetus noticed. He shrugged. 'Went to Gonzaga,' he said. 'I'm not proud of it. Anyway, there's no paper, so I go next door to the office. Paper. Pen. Where *are* they? I have to riffle through half a dozen shagging drawers. By the time I get back he's in no fit condition to sign anything.' Foetus drained his glass and poured another. 'Thing is, though,' he shrugged, 'same result. *It's a till-death-us-do-part-type-thing, Foet.* Rich is dead, contract null and void. So I put the chair back under him. No point sticking around. Vamoose. End of the foregoing.' He took a quick slurp and plonked his glass on the table. 'Anyway, this movie –'

And maybe it was the drink, or the concentration required to finish his gripping tale, but his eyes suddenly muddied over and Foetus fell, face first, into his untouched stew. Hayden wiped a dollop of gravy from the screen of his phone and pocketed it. He lifted Foetus' mobile gingerly off the table and flicked through the texts till he found the Foetus/Rich trail. Foetus/Rich, Foetus/Rich, Foetus/Rich. And this: *not sure killing your agent was such a good idea, darling xxx mater.* It was all there. All the evidence Hayden needed. So he pocketed that too.

He was about to slip out when the waitress arrived back at the table with three friends. Several *Oh my great golly goshes! Is that really him*s? *He is so sexy*s. Odd how the back of an Irishman's head stuck in a plate of cold stew is so appealing to people who don't have to live with it. It calls out, I suppose, to their romantic side. The drink. The accursed craic. The sheer fucking poetry of it all.

And yes, the stew did come out of a tin.

# 26

Back, past the fireworks; the bonfires; the burning, yet again, of a man who was already dead, to Wolfe's. The place was a tip. Wolfe Swift lay on the sofa, comatose. Bit like Foetus, but face up, no stew. Wolfe was obviously smashed. Every so often he'd mumble something or snore violently. He was cradling a bottle of Uncle Eddie's *Sweet Ambrosia*, driblets staining his T-shirt as he breathed heavily in, heavily out. The floor was littered with bottles, while Rusty, traumatised by the relentless explosions outside in the November night, cowered at the foot of the sofa. An open toolbox sat nearby, a few tools strewn about on the floor among the bottles. Wolfe was still busy on backstory. Hayden was relieved, at this stage, that he only wrote the stuff. But what struck him was – he had to admit it – how perfect Wolfe was at playing him. His portrayal was uncanny. Hardly a portrayal at all. He *was* him. He could see it with absolute certainty now: he'd been so, so wrong about Marina. Marina had been faithful to their mutual love; she'd simply consummated it with the wrong Hayden. He'd go back to Dublin to find her. As soon as his script was finished he'd go back. No text. No build-up. Just back.

This thought spurred him on with renewed energy. He placed the two mobiles on his desk and opened his laptop for a quick blast at 'his' new project, *Ravishing*. Great idea, and the sooner he got it to Julius Okeke the sooner the second phase of his brilliant career would kick in. One small task, though, before he got started. Pointer's number. He had it in his wallet. He phoned it. Short pause.

'DCI Pointer. Murder at the Met. How may I help?'

'Glad you could take the call, Detective Chief Inspector. It's –'

'Don't tell me. How's the painting and decorating, Pat?'

'Something has cropped up, Detective Chief Inspector. Something of interest.' Then, and he really couldn't help himself, 'The painting and decorating is a hobby, by the way. I'm writing a film script, actually.'

'Knew you was a bit fly, Pat.' said Pointer. 'Given the swanky address and so forth. Any part for a suave cop? Only I was thinking of whatsisname.'

'The very man,' said Hayden. 'Perfect. I'll check his availability. The reason I called –'

'Ah yes. On you go.'

'Let me put it this way. I think I can help you to clear up an outstanding case. I've located the perp.'

'Intriguing, Pat,' said Pointer. 'Not fantasy murder is it? You wouldn't believe the time I've wasted on wannabe cops.'

'On the contrary. You've already got the corpse. It's –'

'Hold it right there, Pat. We at the Met like a bit of intrigue. Hmmn. Tell you what. I'm dropping in to HMP Belmarsh to check up on Little Mr Lawrie. Bit of an incident, so to speak. Something about over-zealous fans in the communal shower. Inmates, mostly. Couple of guards. Baton. Cake of coal tar soap. Perfect scenario for one of his little jokes. Not that he's in any fit state to write it.'[29]

Pause for a response. Hayden knew the drill. 'Very –'

'Droll?' Pointer chuckled modestly. 'We do our best, Pat, but leave it to the professionals *I* say.' Hayden said nothing. Pointer coughed to fill the void. 'Back to business, Pat. I take it you're still domiciled at your present address? I'll pop round as soon as we've established cause of death. Sad business. Won't do his book sales any harm though, eh? Oh, and we could maybe have

---

[29] Interesting coda from Stern on Little Jimmy's breakout rape joke: 'A joke punches up or it punches down. This one, however, doubles back and shoots itself in the face.' And so it came to pass. RIP Jimmy.

a quick word about your fillum while we're at it. Fillum, Pat. Eh? Fillum?' Pause for another solo chuckle. 'Catch you later, Pat. Two hours tops.'

Hayden put the mobile down, made a soothing mug of hot chocolate, and was soon lost in his new script. I say script. Synopsis. Wise move. Start with the story. Exactly the same story I'd developed all those years ago. As already mentioned, it received a shock-horror response from the film world at the time: *you can't do that!* But it's a dark satire on modern privilege, I said. Glamorous woman gets transported back to famine-era Ireland. She sees the effects of starvation on the peasant population but, and here's the twist, returns to the present and opens a restaurant for weight-watch fanatics: *1847*. No kitchen, no menu, no food. Huge success. The end.

Fair enough. Great idea, I was told, but the famine? Comedy? Come *on*. So I shelved it. I know, I know, I've mentioned this before; but it still rankled, and as Hayden fired into his synopsis I began to get little flashbacks. My past. The stand-up wasn't going too well. Too Level Five-ish. Example:

*I first decided to become a comedian when I was at school.*

*A small child, threatened with violence, says something funny.*

*So any time I saw a small child –*

*'Oi!'*

*Soon as I'd collected enough good one-liners...*

*I quit teaching.*

Bit of an acquired taste, granted, but worse than the stand-up issue, I wasn't getting anywhere with my scripts. On the back of the *Ravishing* rejection I'd been offered a gag-writing job on *Darby O'Gill and the Little People Two*. I was also, I freely admit, overindulging in what I believe are called spirituous liquors. To-kill-the-pain type thing. It was the done thing for the artistic community in those days. The liquid breakfast. I may have railed on, to anyone who would listen, about the unfairness of – well, as it turned out, the unfairness of being ahead of my time.[30]

I also got flashbacks to a very young Hayden McGlynn, desperate to get a foothold in comedy, and hanging on my every word. Watching me perform. Learning the craft. Listening as I recited the plot of *Ravishing* in my cups and storing it away until Ping! Out, several years later, it popped.

One must try to be philosophical, I suppose. And he'd made one interesting change. My script had one heroine, his script three; the Merrie Spinsters to the life. Spot on. If only they'd been around for my version. I was marvelling at the sheer perfection of the central idea, having totally forgotten it in the intervening years, when Foetus' mobile buzzed on Hayden's desk. He ignored it. It wouldn't be for him anyway. The call went on to answering service. Seconds later Wolfe's foundation-shaking snores and the ever-present Guy Fawkes Night explosions were interrupted by a loud rapping on the door. The mobile went again. More rapping. Not Pointer, surely. Too early, and besides, the rapping sounded angry. The letter flap went up.

'You've got my mobile, you bollix. I phoned it on the Aussie bird's lady phone and I can hear it from out here. Jesus, I'm going to have to shag her now and it's all your fucking fault. Hello-o-o! I know you're in there. Listen, I don't know what you're trying to pull but it won't work. I'm warning you. I've got previous.' Short pause. Then a little boy voice. 'Please. I shouldn't've said those things. And anyway, those texts to Rich were, like – I didn't *mean* them.' No response. Pleading wasn't working. Another short pause and back to furious. 'I know what you're up to. You set me up, you devious fucking fuck.'

Hayden sipped his hot chocolate, which had lost its soothing heat. He put the mug down to reverberating *fuck*s. Foetus didn't sound as if he was going away any time soon, which didn't particularly bother Hayden; in fact, it would suit him perfectly

---

[30] Mort De'Ath Syndrome.

if he stuck around till Pointer arrived. The interminable noise from every angle, however, did.

The raps, the explosions, the snores, were hardly conducive to finishing the synopsis. And Rusty added to the mix with a plaintive, shell-shocked dog-wail. Rusty. Gentle, trusting, mentally troubled Rusty, still cowering next to Wolfe. Traumatised. Hayden went over and stroked him on his pitiful, trembling head while Wolfe, arms splayed, one foot over the back of the sofa, snored loudly on.

'There there, little feller,' said Hayden. 'Let's go down the wine cellar, eh? That nice detective won't be here for a while, so come on. Bit of peace and quiet in the cellar. Good dog.'

He went back to his desk and grabbed his laptop, mobile and mug. Hold on. The hot chocolate had gone cold and so, without knowing exactly why he did it, he put the mug down, went over to Wolfe Swift and eased the bottle of *Sweet Ambrosia* from his drunken embrace as Foetus continued to roar through the letterbox. The aroma wafted seductively up his nose. Hayden turned back to Rusty, who stared at him with big, sad eyes.

'Come on, old pal.' Hands full, he went over to the cellar door and bent to put the bottle on the floor; but the door was ajar, so he stood back up and prised it open with his foot. 'Down you go,' he said, but Rusty stayed where he was. Pitiful, trembling, confused. No point trying to coax him, so best to take his work stuff downstairs and come back up for Rusty. Carry him down if necessary. The seductive aroma of *Sweet Ambrosia* tickling his nostrils, he flicked the vermilion light on with his elbow and stepped, tentatively, inside – as a text pinged in.

He glanced at it as his left foot felt for the step.

*You? Me? No Us? xxx*

\*

Foetus was too busy banging and ranting to notice the police car turning into Leverton Street. He didn't notice it double-parking outside. Or the heavy tread of leather shoes. The hand on the shoulder, however, did it. Foetus stood up with a jerk. Too late to hide, though, so he lounged drunkenly against the door and feigned blasé.

'Visiting our old pal Pat, are we?' said Pointer. 'Stick together you Paddies, eh?' Pointer fondled his lapels. 'Here on business m'self. I believe the aforementioned Pat may have information leading to the apprehension of person or persons unknown for crime or crimes equally unknown.' Blasé fled. Not that Pointer noticed. 'Tried knocking, have we?' He rapped on the door and stood back. 'Your catchphrase,' he said. 'Termonfeckin. I've booked me and the missus in for a fortnight in the spring. Could drop in on your old mum if you fancy. You know the drill. "Big fans of your little boy. He makes us laugh." I'm sure she'd like that, your old mum. Vindication of her decision to have you in the first place I would have thought.'

Foetus stood transfixed. Pointer was trying to catch him off guard. Wasn't that what they all did? He'd have to be careful. Very, very careful. 'I'm not from Termonfeckin *as such*,' he said. 'It's, like, a good comedy name, plus it's a sort of rhythm thing.'

Detective Chief Inspector Pointer gave him a quizzical look. 'Not sure I'm with you there, Pat,' he said. 'Hold on.' He cleared his throat theatrically. 'Ahem. Ready? *Hey fella, where you from?*'

'Clondalkin,' said Foetus. 'See? The *yow* doesn't work.'

'Fascinating,' said Pointer. 'This is why you do comedy and I stick to murder.' Foetus froze in his own guilt. Pointer looked perplexed. 'So, what about your old mum?'

'What about her? Oh, that. She lives in Stevenage.'

'My hometown,' said Pointer. 'Shame. I could have popped in last time I was up.'

He bunched his fist to rap on the door again. It opened. A totally inebriated Hayden swayed in the doorway, tried to focus, failed, and staggered back into the room. Pointer followed him in. Hayden – Wolfe?! – wound his way back to the sofa, flopped down and resumed snoring.

'Dear oh dear, Pat,' said Pointer. 'Bit squiffy, are we?' He turned to Foetus. 'He phoned me, what, can't be more than an hour ago. Totally compost mentis, as we gardeners are wont to say.'

Pointer expected a laugh but got nothing; Foetus had a feeling of dark foreboding and bad puns were of no comfort. Pointer got back to business and gave the room a quick once-over.

'Curious. Looks like a bit of a drinking session.' He spotted Rusty, who was cowering by the cellar door, whining. 'Ah. Cellar door open! Light on! Could be something, could be nothing.' He gave Rusty a perfunctory pat on the head and peered in. 'Now this is interesting. Observe the ladder. One of the rungs appears to have snapped. Bit of DIY gone wrong by the looks of it. We also have what appears to be a dead body below if the smashed skull is anything to go by. Odd place to put a beer crate. Case of the drink killing him in the end, eh?' He looked back at Foetus, who had used the fact that Pointer's back was turned to pocket his mobile phone from Hayden's desk.

'Nice one,' said Foetus, who suddenly felt a whole lot better.

As did Detective Chief Inspector Ronnie Pointer. That simple 'nice one' from Foetus was a vindication of his mirth-making skills at last. And from a comedy hero at that! Might take a few lessons. Try his hand. Could be the very thing. Chuffed, he glanced over at the snoring figure on the sofa. 'No sign of foul play as far as I can see, Pat,' he said. 'Your namesake must have been a bit sozzled when he phoned. Might be a lesson for you there. Go easy on the booze.' He glanced back down to the cellar floor. 'The amount of people who come to a bad end down cellars. Some of 'em, I kid you not, the result of foul play. Course we don't have the resources, Pat. Seal 'em up *I* say. And here's another thing. Pat over there, our friend here down the cellar. Looks like they might be twins.' He turned back to Wolfe, snorting happily on the sofa. 'Nothing complicated about this case after all, Pat. We appear to have a body. We also appear to have cause of death.'

Foetus made his way, tentatively, to the front door.

'Off, are we?' Pointer called.

'Late night gig,' lied Foetus, prising a clump of mutton from his fringe.

'Comedy never sleeps, eh? Well, mind how you go. Oh, and where was it you're from, again?'

'Clondalkin,' said Foetus.

Detective Chief Inspector Pointer thought about this for a moment. 'You're right,' he said. 'It's got to be Termonfeckin.'

# 27

Foetus may have got away with murder by omission. Lucky break. The moment had passed, however, on his new American agent. His star went quickly on the wane and he took over as compère on the twenty-seventh series of afternoon TV quiz show *Only Quotin'*. But this is not about Foetus.

Pointer went to Termonfeckin anyway. Why waste a good catchphrase? I often thought he was the prototype for the smash hit Sunday evening cop show, *Mind How You Go*, which harks back to the London of a kinder, gentler time.[31] In series one he misses the German spy-cum-paedophile ring operating out of Scotland Yard and solves a bicycle pump theft instead. But this is not about Pointer either.

Hayden's synopsis of *Ravishing* was actually pretty good. To his credit, he'd added a few details I'd never have thought of, including the three-women-in-one touch. Nice. He'd also discovered the truth of the age-old adage, *The secret to life is being knocked down seven times and getting up six.* But this is not about Hayden any more.

It's about me.

\*

Julius Okeke looked up from the script he wasn't reading. 'You barge in here,' he said. 'You slap this down on my desk. You say you haven't stolen it.' He drummed his fingers on the gleaming oak. 'You're pretty cocky for an older guy.'

---

[31] The Blitz.

'My middle name,' I said. 'Cockademus. And let's say I nicked it back.' I leaned forward in my seat. 'Look. You had a meeting with Hayden McGlynn this morning. 11.42. He couldn't make it.'

'Any idea why?'

'He's dead. It's now 11.43. Might I suggest we move on to other business?'

'You didn't kill him, by any chance?' said Julius Okeke.

'You're wasting *my* time,' I said. 'You're wasting *your* time.' I patted the script. 'I've finished this. I have more where it came from. My motto?' I gave him the hard stare. 'Let me tell you a little story,' I said. 'I was brought up in Clontarf. We didn't have a goat. My father didn't go away. But Clontarf is one of the last bastions of privilege in North Dublin, surrounded as it is by darkest Coolock and equally darkest Killester. My point? I was born into privilege and I fully intend to keep it that way. So, back to that motto.' I leaned forward to drive my point home. *'Overfeed The Beast.'*

Julius smiled approvingly and fingered his fob. He was going to compliment me on my ruthlessness. Call me his friend. Tell me a story about his character-building childhood in the Horn of Africa. You can always tell. The Bonding Session. Four minutes left and the script still sat there, alone and unloved. I was about to point this out and suggest that I could always take my business elsewhere, when the door flew open and Melanie 'Bud' Schultz charged in. I half expected a follow-up burst of machine gun fire. Not this time, though. She had something to say.

'This is driving me crazy,' she barked. 'You're his agent, Julie baby, so hit me. *Invisible Woman.* It *was* Wolfe, right?' She turned to me. 'That was *not* Sherilee Lewis. No way. Back me up here!'

I couldn't. I didn't. Julius Okeke did the what-can-I-say hand thing. 'Face it, Melanie. Nobody knows anything. Now, when I was growing up in the Horn of Africa –'

Bud was furious. 'Correction one. Not the lady name. Melanie is dead to me.' He whacked the table with a tiny fist. 'Bud. Always Bud. Correction two. Movie world? Bud is God. God knows everything. There's no way that was Sherilee Lewis. Compren? Oh, and fuck the Horn of Africa. You, my friend, are from East Dulwich.'

'If I may be permitted to interject,' I interjected.

Bud cut across me. 'You are *not* permitted to interject,' he counter-interjected in a curiously macho-female way. 'Plus I fucked your mother.'

And he was gone.

'Interesting man,' said Julius Okeke. 'She has a fine mind.' He glanced at his fob watch. 'It is now 11.58 point 5. I have decided to extend the meeting. You have 90 seconds to sell yourself.'

'Does that include the bit after you said 11.58 point 5?' I replied wittily.

'Yes. It also included your witty riposte. And my response to same.'

Seventy-two seconds to sell myself. Enough with the banter. I leaned across the desk.

'My other motto,' I said. Two mottoes? He looked at me with a new respect. I hit him while I was hot. '*Comfort the comfortable, afflict the afflicted. That's where the big money is.*' I could see what he was thinking. Naked capitalism in a soundbite? I can work with this man.

# 28

Hayden's funeral. I was so busy on different projects I almost missed it. A script was needed for *Ravishing*. I was on it. Ideas poured out.[32] I was on them. Writing about writing is passé. I'm off it.

I wanted to attend the funeral for obvious reasons. I stood at the back of the room as Hayden had done, oh, it seemed a lifetime ago. It *was* a lifetime ago, come to think of it. His. I examined the backs of people's heads as the humanist celebrant droned on. Very moving, it goes without saying, but I wasn't engaging, so I took to counting the wizened old heads, aunts mainly, scattered and bobbing about in what was a pretty full house. The humanist stopped, the heads bobbed on. The coffin went slowly in. The odd cough; a plaintive, perfectly timed dog howl; then silence. Reverence.

A mournful melody from a lone fiddle.

The fiddle wept to a halt.

A breezy voice from the back. 'Okay, guys. It's a wrap.'

Everyone started shuffling out as if they were still filming. I stayed on. The coffin trundled back from the incinerator and a couple of teckies set about it with electric screwdrivers. The lid was removed. Nothing. Pause. The same voice from the back. 'Wolfe?' Pause. 'Wolfe?' Pause. 'Shit. Get a doctor, someone. And lock the fucking doors.'

---

[32] Example: *Lil J*. Zeitgeisty script about a comedian forced to live his own jokes.

Lucky break. One of the remaining extras was a retired doctor with the acting bug. She stood over the coffin and felt Wolfe's pulse.

'Technically dead,' she said.

Two burly men stepped up from the back. The Pope twins, Grego the cab driver's brothers. JP and Benny. Let's say they convinced me to write them in. They brushed in front of the doctor.

'Give us a look, darlin',' said Benny. 'We know fucken dead when we see ih.'

JP was straight in. 'Thah's my line, ya fucken bollix.'

'Do you mind?' snapped the doctor. 'Kindly step back. This instant.' She dismissed them with a cursory wave and turned to the director. 'You didn't, by any chance, embalm him?'

'Up to a point,' he mumbled apologetically. 'Wolfe insisted.'

The doctor shook her head. 'Not good,' she said, 'but – hold on. I'm getting something.'

She lifted Wolfe's head gently from its resting place and slapped his cheeks hard.

Nothing.

Nothing twice.

Then? A facial spasm from truly The Greatest Actor Of This Or Any Other Age, recently technically deceased, and his eyes started to twitch. They opened slowly and tried to focus as Wolfe sat blearily up and blinked back to life. 'Give me a minute,' he said. 'I think I've just met God.' A nervous laugh from the director, the doctor, the teckies, JP, Benny and, finally, me. 'No, seriously,' said Wolfe. 'Long white beard. Robe. He said, "Your time has not yet come, you haven't played *Me* yet." I knew He was God by the capital M.' He looked momentarily confused. 'Come to think of it,' he said, 'He wasn't a He. The robe was actually a dress. I thought confused sexuality here, but no. "I know what you're thinking, Wolfe," She said. "How come the long white beard? Think about it. I evolved over scrillions of years. Great title, by the way; *The Scrillion-Year-Old Woman.*

Want to take it down? Whatever. Anyway, after the first million or so, you start to get a bit of facial hair. You're vain. You deal with it. Couple of million more and Y[33]ou're thinking, *Now where did I put that razor? Oh, what the hell, it's not about looks.* My point? The beard evolved. And I still know what you're thinking. Why don't You let people know You're a woman?"' Exactly what *I* was thinking, come to think of it. Exactly what everyone was thinking. Wolfe paused – brilliant timing, but what else would you expect? – and continued. '"Simple," She said. "I don't want to alienate My fan base." Then, and maybe it's because I laughed, She told me a joke. Couldn't make head or tail of it to be honest. Can't even remember what it was. Didn't seem to bother Her, though. "Don't worry about it, Wolfie. Level Six." And She was gone. End of death experience. And here I am.'

A still slightly dazed Wolfe stepped out of the coffin; the coffin still smouldering, Wolfe lightly singed. 'See you all later down the Nautical Buoy,' he said and stumbled, still blinking, towards the exit.

I was left to reflect that Emeritus Professor Larry Stern had been right all along. The greatest joke ever. Level Six. And we'll never know what it was. Or ever understand it.

In this life at least.

*

I followed Wolfe out. I wanted words, but you know how it is. I was surrounded as soon as I left the crematorium. The Merrie Spinsters. Hayden's beloved aunts.

'Exactly like Hayding's funerdle, Een.'

'You could almost say his funerdle was in the way of being an audishing.'

'We couldn't make it for the real ting, unfortunously –'

---

[33] Capital Y. God, remember?

'– being as how we were reliving our glory days on the Left Bank for our fortcoming documentary on the Arts Channel at the time –'

'– but this was more than recompensatious.'

They were getting worse, there was no denying it. Having said that, they did have a combined age touching three hundred. Three seventy-five if you include the Merries, who had decided to stay in character. So, come to think of it, touching six.

'We've read trew your manuscript, Een. You've got us to the life. But, and it's one gynormous but –'

'Langwidge, Florrie.'

'Dottie. You couldn't let Hayding get the glory, Een, so you done away wit him, like he done away wit his Uncle Eddie, *aka* his very own Daddy, all doze munts ago.'

'In a funny sort of way, Een, Hayding was the son you never had.'

I was about to put in a word for the defence but what was the point? Six nonagenarian aunts? You try it.

'We know you done it, Een. We know you killed him. You were the brains anyway. There was always something a bit –'

'– what's the word? –'

'– *outré* about you, if you don't mind us saying.'

I did. Nothing to be done, though. They'd already said it.

'But don't worry, Een. We'll look after you, because in a funny sort of way we're all your mammies now.'

Wolfe seemed to be on the verge of leaving, and I really did want a private word.

'Good to know, ladies,' I said. 'Six mammies, could be a record; but I really must dash.'

'One final ting, Een. We've read *The Unbridled Ego: Men in Comedy*, by the estimable Professor Stern.'

'Larry the Love Doctor to us, Een, and what a –'

'Stick to the subject, Dorrie.'

'Veronica. Which is?'

'*The Ego Unleashed.* We tought, that's Hayding, that is, and that's Een too. That's what makes them great men and us mere figments of the imaginayshing.' She glinted mischievously. 'Or maybe,' she giggled, 'it's the udder way round. Maybe *you're* figments of *our* imaginayshing.'

The other aunts all rounded on her. Hissing.

'That, Dottie, is strictly confidentuous.'

'Leave the poor boy to his dreams.'

They turned to me en masse.

'And speaking of dreams, Een, congratulayshings on your book –'

'– which now draws inexorably towards its joyous, uplifting close.'

'A work of comedy fit to sit wit the greats.'

'So go fort, Een the Outré.'

'Divide and multiply.'

And they were off. Giggle giggle giggle. Giggle giggle giggle giggle giggle. If the wind is in the wrong direction, or my dreams take an ugly turn, I think I can hear them still. *The Unholy Fates.* I took advantage of the absence of words – even *they* can't giggle and converse at the same time – to race after Wolfe.

Wind back a bit first. Interesting thought, that I was merely a figment of the three aunts' collective imagination. It certainly sounded plausible and came as something of a relief. If there's another book, they can write the bloody thing themselves. No time for that now, though. A top-of-the-range film-star car pulled up beside Wolfe. He was about to be whisked off. I'd have to be quick but Christ! Another interruption. What's that line in screenwriter manuals about metaphorical beer barrels blocking our hero's path? The Merrie Spinsters needed a word too. With me. Out of character.

'Listen, Macker,' they said. '*You* –'

'I know, I know,' I said. 'I'm the man. Got to go. But *Ravishing.* Three parts. You. You. You. Wrote 'em special. Oh, and hold the blow job. I'm spoken for.'

I was off again. I'd almost reached Wolfe when, slight twist, a statuesque and stunning woman wound down the window of the film-star car. I was wrong about the whisk bit.

'Sherilee,' said Wolfe. 'Now there's a pleasant surprise.'

'Keep it down,' beamed Sherilee. 'I'm travelling incognito.'

Wolfe kissed her on both cheeks. 'That would explain the Bugatti,' he said. 'And listen. You saved my life at the Oscars. The debt shall be repaid a thousandfold.'

'Oh, shoot, girlfriend,' said Sherilee. 'I took it as an acting job. Besides, easiest award *I* ever got. Plus it's got me my next part. *Dook Wayne: Imperial Wiz*. First KKK grand-mistress of colour. Hood acting. Turns out Dook is short for Dookess.'

I was lost in admiration for Wolfe. He'd passed on the greatest accolade his profession can bestow. Wolfe Swift was married to the work, not the fame. *He* knew he'd done it. That was enough.

As Sherilee vroomed off I raced after a swiftly retreating Wolfe. 'Wolfe!'

He turned to face me, weary from all that character work. He really didn't need this. 'Oh, it's you,' he said. 'Thanks. Great script.'

'Never mind about that,' I said. 'The past is the past. Let the dead bury their dead. Move on.' Do we have to? He didn't say that, but he would have if I'd let him. 'Hear me out,' I said. 'Well-known-fact update. There are seven basic plots. This, my friend, is number eight.' Hyperbole? My other middle name. I thought about a dramatic pause. No time. 'Perfect vehicle for the right screen great.'

Wolfe sighed wearily. Too cool for compliments.

'Okay,' he said. 'Okay. You've got –'

'I know, I know,' I said. '90 seconds.' I was off. 'Pitch. *Back To The Womb*, right?' The Swift antennae were up. I knew I had him. 'Murder mystery. The MacDonagh Brothers. Bitter rival identical twin detectives from Boston, convinced they're Irish. Female victim. Isn't it always? One brother solves the case, the other murders him and takes the credit. Neat, hoh?' Wolfe was transfixed, as I knew he would be. 'We're talking fratricide,' I said, 'but here's the twist. On his distraught mother's deathbed' – I paused to let the mother word resonate – 'the living brother looks her in the eye' – I paused to let the image resonate – 'and promises to find out who killed the dead one! Twin atones for killing fellow twin. A chance for familial closure! A chance,' I all but declaimed, 'for the healing power of truth!' Eighty-six seconds. I paused for the final two. 'Well?'

Wolfe was speechless, as I knew he would be. Ninety seconds. He decided to extend the pitch. More speechless. Then actor Wolfe kicked in. Magnificently assured, yet curiously vulnerable with it. 'So – where's my part?'

'The masterstroke!' I said. 'Both brothers. And –' a double beat for effect '– the mother.'

He paused.

Stroked his chin.

Went deep, deep inside himself. Deep, deep inside his mother. Transported back to the womb.

Then he fixed me with those eyes. Those lupine eyes.

'Let's do it!'

# 29

I sit at the writing desk in Wolfe's house. I say Wolfe's. Let me amend that. My house. It came with the dog. Rusty sits at my feet, looking up adoringly and nuzzling my knee. I'll take him out for a walk in a while, and Marina will drop by later, but first there's the small matter of the script.

The sun slants across Eddie's statue in pride of place on the lawn.

The statue – it's mid-day precisely – looks uncannily like God.

And She smiles down on me and all my works.

Everlastingly.

# ACKNOWLEDGMENTS

Thanks to all at Bluemoose, publishers of *Sloot* and now *Hewbris*. Immortality guaranteed, I would have thought. Special thanks to Annie Warren for her excellent editing, Magi Gibson for her close involvement at every stage of the book's development, and the two dedicatees: Davy Macpherson, a very special brother; Arnold Brown, a very special friend.